Michael Underwood and The Murder Room

>>> This title is part of The Murder Room, our series dedicated to making available out-of-print or hard-to-find titles by classic crime writers.

Crime fiction has always held up a mirror to society. The Victorians were fascinated by sensational murder and the emerging science of detection; now we are obsessed with the forensic detail of violent death. And no other genre has so captivated and enthralled readers.

Vast troves of classic crime writing have for a long time been unavailable to all but the most dedicated frequenters of second-hand bookshops. The advent of digital publishing means that we are now able to bring you the backlists of a huge range of titles by classic and contemporary crime writers, some of which have been out of print for decades.

From the genteel amateur private eyes of the Golden Age and the femmes fatales of pulp fiction, to the morally ambiguous hard-boiled detectives of mid twentieth-century America and their descendants who walk our twenty-first century streets, The Murder Room has it all. >>>

The Murder Room
Where Criminal Minds Meet

themurderroom.com

T0352496

Michael Underwood (1916–1992)
Michael Underwood (the pseudonym of John Michael Evelyn) was born in Worthing, Sussex and educated at Christ Church College, Oxford. He was called to the Bar in 1939 and served in the British army during World War Two. He returned to work in the Department of Public Prosecutions until his retirement in 1976, and wrote almost 50 crime novels informed by his career in the law. His five series characters include Sergeant Nick Atwell and lawyer Rosa Epton, of whom is was said by the *Washington Post* that she 'outdoes Perry Mason'.

By Michael Underwood

Simon Manton

Murder on Trial (1954)

Murder Made Absolute (1955)

Death on Remand (1956)

False Witness (1957)

Lawful Pursuit (1958)

Arm of the Law (1959)

Cause of Death (1960)

Death by Misadventure (1960)

Adam's Case (1961)

The Case Against Philip
   Quest (1962)

Girl Found Dead (1963)

The Crime of Colin Wise (1964)

The Anxious Conspirator (1956)

Richard Monk

The Man Who Died on
   Friday (1967)

The Man Who Killed Too
   Soon (1968)

Martin Ainsworth

The Shadow Game (1970)

Trout in the Milk (1971)

Reward for a Defector (1973)

The Unprofessional Spy (1975)

Rosa Epton

A Pinch of Snuff (1974)

Crime upon Crime (1980)

Double Jeopardy (1981)

Goddess of Death (1982)

A Party to Murder (1983)

Death in Camera (1984)

The Hidden Man (1985)

Death at Deepwood
   Grange (1986)

The Injudicious Judge (1982)

The Uninvited Corpse (1987)

Dual Enigma (1988)

A Compelling Case (1989)

A Dangerous Business (1990)

Rosa's Dilemma (1990)

The Seeds of Murder (1991)

Guilty Conscience (1992)

Nick Atwell

The Juror (1975)

Menaces, Menaces (1976)

The Fatal Trip (1977)

Murder with Malice (1977)

Crooked Wood (1978)

Standalone titles

A Crime Apart (1966)

Shem's Demise (1970)

The Silent Liars (1970)

Anything but the Truth (1978)

Smooth Justice (1979)

Victim of Circumstance (1979)

A Clear Case of Suicide (1980)

Hand of Fate (1981)

The Silent Liars

Michael Underwood

An Orion book

Copyright © Isobel Mackenzie 1970

The right of Michael Underwood to be identified as the author of this work has been asserted in accordance with the Copyright, Designs and Patents Act 1988.

This edition published by
The Orion Publishing Group Ltd
Orion House
5 Upper St Martin's Lane
London WC2H 9EA

An Hachette UK company
A CIP catalogue record for this book is available from the British Library

ISBN 978 1 4719 0817 1

www.orionbooks.co.uk

To Julian Symons

To Julian Symons

PART I

'Christopher Joyce Laker, you stand charged with murder, the particulars being that on the 27th February you murdered Gheorge Dimitriu . . . Do you plead guilty or not guilty?'

Of course, he had said 'not guilty'; and so far that was all he had said during his trial which was now entering its third day. He could seldom remember having been so bored as over the past two days and he wondered whether other occupants of the vast dock of Number 1 Court at the Old Bailey had experienced the same unreal sense of detachment in the course of their trials for murder. Crippen or Seddon for example? Or, coming a bit closer in time, Heath or Christie? Had their bottoms been incessantly reminded of the hardness of the chair? Perhaps it was feared that if prisoners were given the same padded upholstery as everyone else in court they might drop off to sleep through the tedium of it all.

Chris Laker smothered a yawn and let his glance roam round the crowded benches. Yes, she was still there keeping vigil, the old girl with iron-grey hair pulled back into a tight bun and dressed in layers of heavy mourning. Always there with her eyes fixed on the dock as he took his place each morning and afternoon; always subjecting him to long periods of intense scrutiny, which he had come to find annoyingly disconcerting.

He had gathered early on that she was the widow of the murdered man. Her daily attendance struck him as curious, bordering on the unnatural. He was not to know that others felt the same and had, for their own various reasons, tried to dissuade her from attending. But she had brushed all opposition aside, including that of her son, Peter, who was a witness in the case and who would very much have preferred his mother to stay away.

'I shall never rest until I know the truth of Gheorge's

death,' she defiantly told the World, in her guttural English, as she set out each day to fasten her eyes on the young man charged with his murder . . .

Christopher Joyce Laker, aged twenty-seven, 5 feet 11 inches tall and weighing 11 stone. Slim, bespectacled and with thick dark brown hair covering a head which his girl-friend, Janey, professed to be his most interesting feature. What she meant was that it had been the shape of his head which had, so to speak, led her to his bed in the first place. Thereafter, she had found additional reasons for staying in it.

Christopher *Joyce* Laker. It had taken the law to dig out his second name, and public reminder of it had come as an ugly jab in the ribs. It wasn't even as if it had any literary significance. It was simply his mother's maiden name which had, in one heedless moment, been tied round his neck at baptism.

It would be false to pretend that it had been the cause of his drift away from home and the world of his parents, but it had certainly persuaded him at an early age that there could never be any real understanding between himself and a mother and father who had connived in such a purblind decision. He knew they were now suffering deep shame at their son standing trial for murder, and he was genuinely sorry that this was so. On the other hand, they had never begun to understand the shame he had experienced at school with such a name. Inevitably it had leaked out and he had at first been mercilessly teased. Only a determined use of fists and feet had saved him from utter humiliation. Feet, in particular, as his long legs had given him a specially effective reach when connecting with his tormentors' behinds.

It wasn't, though, that he hated his parents. He just had nothing in common with them and hadn't had since he first began making decisions for himself. He still kept in touch with them in a casual way, though contact was infrequent and the result only of the residue of a sense of duty whose existence he appeared to deny. It was much the same on their side, save that *they* regarded their sense of duty as natural and virtuous.

Both of them had visited him in prison while he had been awaiting trial, but they had been uncomfortable visits which he could have dispensed with. The more so, since he had declined to tell them anything about the case or how he had come to be charged with murder, and his parents – his mother, at any rate – had clearly hoped that this might be the occasion of filial confession, followed by reconciliation.

'Is there nothing you want to tell us, Chris?' she had asked awkwardly on their first visit after his arrest.

'Tell you?' he had repeated in a puzzled tone, knowing quite well what she meant.

'About . . . about your trouble,' she had said, biting her lip to keep back the tears.

He had shaken his head. 'Don't worry, Mum, I'm going to be all right,' he said, and had let it go at that.

He had observed his father sitting in court on the first morning of the trial and knew he must have taken half a day's leave from the Ministry of Transport where he was a Senior Executive Officer in a section which dealt with road accident statistics. Chris couldn't conceive a drearier life, and the whole rigmarole of civil service protocol filled him with amused contempt. The very absurdity of having to fill in a chit in order to have a morning off from work . . . Come to that the whole drab business of a regular job! Anyhow, he was relieved when his father had failed to put in any further appearances, which could only have been an embarrassment to each of them. He had heard prosecuting counsel open the case against his son, so now knew as much as anyone else . . . Well, as much as any other informed observer of the case.

Chris let his glance wander to the witness-box where a small, mousy-looking man seemed to have been in occupation since time began. Looking as though at any moment he might be completely swallowed up inside his overlarge suit, leaving only a medal row of coloured ball-point pens to mark his presence, he gave his evidence in an unimpassioned monotone, which successfully concealed its effect from the unwary. He was Mr Mendip of the Forensic Science Laboratory. He had entered the witness-box the previous afternoon and was now under cross-examination from Chris' counsel, Charles Lynn.

Chris found his evidence reaching new peaks of unreality in a trial which was unreal enough in all conscience. It was quite impossible to associate this painstakingly detailed testimony about chemically analysed fibres and shoe scrapings with anything *he* was supposed to have done. He wanted to spit in their combined faces, judge, jury, counsel, spectators, the lot. To spit and then slip away, leaving them to enact this elaborate charade without him. It irked him to be the selected victim round whom it all revolved.

It wasn't that he was indifferent to the outcome. Nothing could be further from the fact. There had been several nights in prison when he had woken up and experienced genuine terror as his mind peered into the black void which would be his life if he were to be convicted. But with the arrival of a new day, he'd once more been enabled to live for the present and let the future take care of itself. That had always been his way; the reason why he had never settled to a steady job or looked ahead to marriage and children. He knew he was a drifter, but he declined to acknowledge it as an opprobrious term. He worked for as short spells as possible in order to earn enough money with which to amuse himself, to travel and do nothing, to read books on oriental philosophy or to improve his technique as a serious guitarist. It was an intelligent way of life; far more so, he felt, than the rat race in which the majority elected to compete.

He leant forward and rested his chin on his knuckles in an 'Il Penseroso' pose. Might as well do something to try and impress the jury, though twelve more middle-aged, mundane fish out of water he had seldom seen. They might have come straight from his father's Ministry. That was exactly what they resembled, a bunch of minor civil servants. He'd thought so as he had watched them being sworn on the first day. In the circumstances, it was probably as well that he had taken his solicitor's advice to dress appropriately for the occasion.

'Haven't you got a dark suit?' Mr Wells has asked, eyeing him at their first meeting when he was dressed in grubby jeans and a black turtle-neck sweater, which was equally grubby but didn't show it.

'Yes.'

'Good, then I'll have it sent in. Important to make a good impression on the jury. Doesn't do to look like a scruff.'

And so here he was, looking, instead, like a studious bank clerk, in a charcoal grey suit, cream shirt and sober blue tie.

The shirt and tie were new, presents from Janey, who had aided and abetted Mr Wells in his efforts to make his client as presentable as possible.

He hadn't seen Janey since the trial began, though he knew that she was not very far away. Not by any pricking of his thumbs, but because Mr Wells had told him she was waiting outside the courtroom. Waiting until the moment arrived for her to give evidence on his behalf. All witnesses, Mr Wells explained, had to wait out of court so that their evidence was untainted by those who went ahead of them into the box.

Chris had for some time been very much in two minds about her giving evidence at all. If it was really going to help him get off, then the price was worth it. The price being the obligation she was placing him under by so doing. He eschewed obligations, the more especially where girl-friends were concerned. It had been his experience that almost without exception they tried to truss you up with these moral silken cords, hoping you wouldn't notice until the chosen moment – their chosen moment – arrived. He could think of only one girl with whom he'd lived for any time who had not been so and *their* relationship had foundered when she developed compulsive urges to get up in the middle of the night and go and write poetry in the waiting-room of Victoria Station. Sometimes she would be away only two hours, others eight or nine, and on one occasion over twenty-four ... Chris had decided that this was straining even a lax relationship too far.

Certainly he had never been with anyone as long as he had with Janey. It was fifteen months since they'd first met on an escalator at Earls Court Station. The heel of her shoe had become wedged between two slats and she had stepped out of it with a small shriek. Chris, who was behind her, had freed it and handed it to her at the top where she was standing on one leg.

'It's a new pair, too,' she had explained after thanking him.

'Well, no damage has been done, so what's it matter whether they're new or old!' he had remarked.

She had looked at him in surprise.

'Because they *might* have been wrecked, that's why it matters,' she had replied tartly.

'The shoe's not even scratched, so their age has nothing to do with it.' Then before she could make any further retort, he had said quickly, 'Why don't we continue this interesting conversation over a cup of coffee. There's lots more I want to hear about your shoes ...'

When they were seated in Clara's Coffee Shop, he learnt that she was Jane Holland, was twenty years old and the fourth child of a West Country corn merchant. Also that she shared a flat with three other girls and had a job in a small, newly-established literary agency, where she answered the telephone and the door, did some typing, attended to the demands of morning and afternoon tea-brewing, not to mention the packing up of rejected manuscripts and the maintenance of a press-cutting book, in which every reference to the firm's authors was diligently recorded with the application of a great deal of glue. These, Chris gathered, were just her main duties.

Two weeks later, they had set up home together in a top-floor room of a house in one of the dingier streets off the Fulham Road. Over the next fifteen months, they moved five times. Over the same period, Chris had been in work for approximately one-third of the time, while Janey had remained faithful throughout to her literary agency.

When he did work, however, he worked hard, usually on construction sites with extravagant overtime rates of pay, sometimes as a lorry-driver on piece-work with bonuses for every load over the norm. And the norm was dead easy. In between these hectic spells, he lived on fat.

It had not been long before Janey had voiced disapproval.

'You ought to get a regular job,' she had said bluntly when he had been sitting around for a week soon after they'd joined forces.

'Why?'

'Because you ought to.'

'Why?'

'Everyone ought to.'

'Balls! Anyway, I'm not everyone.'

'What'll you do when you get married?'

'That's an irrelevant question.'

'I suppose you'll expect me to support you when your money has run out?'

'I certainly shan't expect you to, but it's more than likely you'll be prepared to. Even want to.'

'Of all the conceit . . . '

He had seized her and, with a laugh, kissed her firmly. 'What else do you expect from someone with such an interesting-shaped head . . . Anyway, I'm not conceited. I'm merely a realist.'

He had several times been ready for her to walk out on him, but she hadn't and the likelihood had receded, despite the further occasional flashpoint.

The fact was that it had been Janey who had made the adjustments, since it was she who was the more afraid of their relationship ending. Chris was fond of her, indeed had become more so with the passage of time, but it was outside his temperament to get too involved with anyone. This was why he'd never offered her any hope of marriage.

Nevertheless, their life had seemed set on a relatively even keel when trouble struck. Trouble which had resulted in his arrest and his present appearance in the dock of the Old Bailey.

It had been two days before that Mr Sherway, one of the Senior Treasury Counsel, had opened the case for the prosecution. He was a small, nut-brown man who managed to bring to his cases a serious, if slightly wry, manner which was wholly untinged by any strain of pomposity. He always gave the impression of being relaxed, even when under forensic pressure, and juries who had, as a result of watching a surfeit of TV courtroom dramas, come to regard barristers as a tribe of pontificating tyrants, could scarcely believe their eyes, still less their ears, when Dick Sherway rose to address them. His style was as conversational as the vast space of Number 1 Court permitted.

'May it please your lordship, members of the jury, in this case I appear for the Crown with my learned friend, Mr Davis, and the accused is represented by my learned friends, Mr Lynn and Mr Vickery.' At this point he gave them a small reassuring smile as if to say, 'Don't be put off by all the mumbo-jumbo.'

'Members of the jury, as you have heard, the accused, Christopher Joyce Laker, stands indicted with the murder of a man named Gheorge Dimitriu. Let me begin by telling you something about Mr Dimitriu. He was sixty-three years old at the time of his death, which took place on the 27th

February this year when someone – the Crown say that it was the accused – shot him in the head at point-blank range.

'But to go back for a few moments to tell you something about the deceased, before I come to the events of 27th February. Mr Dimitriu was a naturalised British subject of Rumanian birth. He had lived in this country since 1947, where over the years he had built up wide business interests, mostly in the field of property development. He was a married man and for the past five years had lived with his wife and only son at Barnet on the northern outskirts of London. You will hear, for such relevance as it has, that it is a large and comfortable house and that its garage accommodated the three cars which the three members of the household owned between them.' His tone was as dry as a water biscuit. 'I mention these details only to give you an idea of the sort of man whose death we're concerned with in this case. A man of substance; but also, members of the jury, a man round whose last movements a shroud of mystery hangs. The Crown are not in a position to explain everything surrounding his death, but they do say that the evidence points strongly to its having been caused by this young man.'

He shot Chris an appraising glance before turning back to the jury.

'There seems to be little doubt, members of the jury, that Mr Dimitriu was in certain ways a secretive man. That is not in itself a particularly unusual facet of human nature, but it does mean in this case that the Crown are unable to satisfy your natural curiosity on one important issue, namely that of motive. That the accused murdered Mr Dimitriu, the Crown hope to prove beyond reasonable doubt. Why he murdered him, they cannot tell you. That is something known only to the murderer and his victim.'

Several members of the jury cast interested glances in Chris' direction, but were met by a look of counter-appraisal.

'But as my lord will direct you in due course, it is never part of the Crown's duty to prove a motive, though of course if one is apparent it frequently helps to explain what is otherwise obscure. Time and time again accused persons are convicted in our Courts even though the prosecution

8

have been unable to adduce any evidence of motive. They are convicted because the facts, and the inferences which must be drawn from them, point clearly to guilt.'

He paused a moment, braced his shoulders and went on: 'Moreover, it is also right that I should tell you that the Crown are unable to link the accused with the deceased, other than by circumstantial evidence. The accused himself has denied all knowledge of Mr Dimitriu. He says, in effect, I didn't kill him, I didn't know him. I'd never even heard of him.

'Members of the jury, the 27th of February fell on a Thursday. It was a dry day – indeed, there had been no rain for over two weeks – but in the evening, which is the time we're concerned with, there was slight mist. Mr Dimitriu arrived home from his office in Park Lane shortly before seven o'clock. He gave every appearance of being his normal self, but he told his wife that he wouldn't be staying in for dinner that evening. But apart from that bald statement, he gave no indication of his plans. It seems that he sat having a drink and reading the evening paper in the drawing-room until about a quarter to eight when he suddenly looked at his watch, got up and left the house without a word. The last his wife saw of him – his son, too, for that matter, since he was also in the house at the time – was driving off in his Rolls-Bentley.'

He paused and turned a page of the notebook propped open in front of him. When he went on, his tone had become brisk and businesslike.

'When by next morning he had failed to return home, the police were informed. About ten o'clock that next day, the Friday, a Mr James Exon was walking through a wood, known as Riches Wood, when he came across Mr Dimitriu's car with, inside, dead in the driver's seat, Mr Dimitriu.

'You will hear in evidence that the car was parked on a little-used track which runs through the wood and that it was about a quarter of a mile off the road and nearly a mile from the nearest house. A lonely spot for somewhere within the built-up area of this great sprawling city. A spot which is about six miles from the home of the deceased. You will note, members of the jury, that I said six miles, but the Crown will call evidence which shows that the car had covered three times that distance between leaving the house at a quarter to eight on Thursday evening and its discovery at ten o'clock the next morning. Within ten minutes of Mr Exon finding it, the police were on the scene. Let me tell you what they found.

'Mr Dimitriu was slumped sideways against the driver's door, his head resting against the lower part of the window. There was a bullet wound in his left temple and a much larger wound in the other temple where the bullet had come out. It had then passed through the car window and embedded itself in a tree about eight feet beyond the car. Round the entry wound there were scorch marks indicating that the muzzle of the weapon had been approximately six inches away from the deceased's head at the time of the shot. Apart from this bullet wound, there were no other marks or signs of injury on the body. Moreover, you will hear that Mr Dimitriu was dressed exactly as when he left the house the previous evening. The pathologist will tell you that he had been dead for between twelve and eighteen hours.'

Mr Sherway bent slightly forward and rested his fingertips on the top of the ledge in front of him.

'On the floor of the car on the passenger's side lay a revolver. A Smith and Wesson .38. It had one spent case in the firing position and three unused bullets in the chamber; indicating that one bullet had been sufficient for the murderer's purpose. There was a single fingerprint on the revolver, members of the jury – and that fingerprint was the accused's.' He made a small, throwaway gesture in Chris' direction, as though there might be some in court still unaware of which was the accused.

'It was the print of his right index finger and it was found in one of the shallow grooves of the cylindrical chamber which holds the bullets. There were no other fingerprints on the revolver, which indicates that the murderer wore gloves when committing the crime. He wore gloves, then, but he overlooked the fact that he had earlier left a print on it when loading or cleaning the revolver. While on this point, I should tell you that the deceased man was not wearing gloves, which rules out the possibility of his having shot himself. Moreover, there is other evidence of an expert nature, with which I needn't trouble you at this stage, showing conclusively that this was murder and not suicide.

'Well, members of the jury, as you will probably have

assumed from your general knowledge about such matters, in the wake of the police came the experts. The pathologist, the scientist from the laboratory, the photographer and the fingerprint officer, whose evidence I've already told you of. But let me just complete what I have to say about his evidence.

'The only identifiable fingerprints on the car itself were those of the deceased. You might have expected to have found prints belonging to the accused, either on the passenger door or in the area of the passenger seat, *unless* the murderer was wearing gloves . . .

'I ought to have told you that both the driver's and front passenger's doors were unlocked when the car was found – the rear doors were, however, locked – and that all the windows were up. The driver's window, as I've already mentioned, had been broken by the passage of the bullet.

'No further fingerprints, then, were found, members of the jury; but something else of great significance was found. Fibres! Fibres adhering to the passenger seat which are identical with fibres from a cardigan belonging to the accused. One of those thick, chunky cardigans with a knitted collar and dark brown in colour. What I would call the colour of old-fashioned treacle toffee, members of the jury, though I have no doubt that it goes under a far more resplendent description than that . . .

'So you have in this car a dead man shot through the head, a revolver from which the fatal bullet was fired and which bears the accused's fingerprint and fibres which are identical with those from a cardigan which he used frequently to wear, and was, moreover, seen to be wearing on the afternoon of that day, the day on which the murder was committed . . .

'And now, members of the jury, the time has come when we must turn our attention to the accused himself.

'Exactly one week after the murder, the police received information which resulted in their calling on the accused at his address, 36 Forton Street in Earls Court. The two officers who went to see him there were Detective Chief Inspector Adams and Detective Sergeant Paget. Mr Adams asked him if he'd known a man named Dimitriu and he said he had not. The Chief Inspector then drew his attention to the murder – it had been fully reported in the press – and

11

the accused said he thought he did remember having read something about it in the papers, but he didn't normally follow reports of crimes and so it hadn't made all that impression on him. He was then asked if he would have any objection to the officers examining his room – it is in fact a one-room flat which he shares with a girl – and he said he had not. In the course of the examination, Chief Inspector Adams took possession, with the accused's consent, of a number of articles of clothing, including the brown cardigan. He was asked about his movements on the evening of 27th February and though he professed slight haziness about where he'd been and when, he was quite adamant that he had been nowhere near Barnet or Riches Wood. He said he had never left the Earls Court area the whole of that day. He added that he was not in employment at that time.

'He was then asked if he would accompany the officers to the police station and, after slight hesitation, he agreed. At the station, he was asked if he possessed a revolver and he said "no". He was asked if he'd ever had one and again he said "no". It was certainly true that the officers had failed to find one when they searched his room, though the Crown say, of course, that was because he'd left it at the scene of the crime.

'He was then asked if he would be prepared to give his fingerprints and, this time, after considerable hesitation, he agreed. Let me explain, members of the jury, that from time to time in the course of a criminal investigation people are asked to co-operate with the police by giving their fingerprints. Those who agree do so on the understanding that the forms will be destroyed once they have served their purpose of eliminating the person concerned from the inquiry.

'Well, the accused gave his fingerprints and then after some further questioning during which he repeated his earlier denials, he left the station. But the next day the same two officers again went to his address and asked him to accompany them back to the station. On arrival there, he was told that the fingerprint on the revolver which killed Mr Dimitriu matched that made by his right index finger. And he was cautioned.

'What the accused then told the police was this. That he did own a revolver, that he had bought it from a workmate on a building site about six months previously and that it had lain unused in a clothing drawer all the time he'd had it. He had now discovered it was missing and could only conclude that it must have been stolen, though he had no idea when that could have happened. He went on to say that he had never had a firearms certificate for it and that was why he had denied ownership when first seen by the police.'

Mr Sherway lowered his eyes and appeared to stare thoughtfully at the back of the head in front of him. Then looking up, he said in his quiet conversational tone, 'Well, members of the jury, it will be for you to weigh that explanation in the light of the evidence as a whole. However, you may well wonder why this young man bought the revolver in the first place, if it was merely to bury it in a drawer full of clothing. More particularly, seeing that he has also admitted that he had acquired four rounds of ammunition with the revolver. And why, even supposing for one moment that his story is true, he felt obliged to deny his ownership. Can you really believe that the mere lack of a firearms certificate was what deterred him?

'Those are questions which you will doubtless keep in mind. Questions to which you will wish to have answers. The Crown say, of course, that the inferences are irresistible. Namely that it was the accused's revolver, fired by him, which ended Mr Dimitriu's life. If not, why the lies, members of the jury, why the lies?'

It was at this point that Chris' attention had first begun to stray. Until that moment he had been following counsel's opening speech with reasonable concentration, even though the extraordinary feeling of detachment was ever with him. But Mr Sherway's 'Why the lies, members of the jury, why te lies?' spoken in a quietly insistent tone, jolted his mind into a sudden uncomfortable review of realities, from which it never returned.

By the time he had completed his reflections on counsel's unpleasant little rhetorical question, the opening was over and the first witness was giving evidence. From then on his attention constantly strayed, not least on account of the protracted tedium of it all. How the law spun everything out! Sometimes they might have been trying the man-in-the-moon for all the notice he received. Sometimes he thought they were, as when judge and counsel embarked on a sort of verbal minuet on whether one of the witnesses'

statements was valid in the light of some clerical omission
from a signed declaration at its end. Anyway, if not exactly
that, it was something equally idiotic.

As he sat listening with half an ear while they picked their
delicate way through a maze of sections and sub-sections, it
had only been the presence of two large prison officers in
the dock with him which prevented his getting up and walking out, as one might walk out of a boring film.

He experienced the same feeling of boredom as he had
on being taken to church when he was a small boy. At least
then, there'd been music and singing and you could always
shunt the hassocks around or pile up hymn books in between times. All he now had to play with was a pencil and a
pad of paper on which he was supposed to make notes of
anything which came to his mind as the trial progressed. The
pad of paper remained blank and looked like continuing
that way. He had heard how some accused were prolific
note-passers and seldom stopped scribbling messages to
their counsel. Whatever else he might be remembered for, it
wouldn't be that!

And so the first morning had passed.

Observing his son in court that day left Mr Laker bewildered, angry and not a little frightened. Bewildered and
frightened because he was unable to comprehend what was
going on in his son's mind. Angry, because he wasn't adopt-
ing the right attitude towards his trial, whatever that should
have been.

It was with bitterness that he returned home in the
evening and described the scene to his wife.

'I don't mind telling you, Gwen, that my stomach turned
right over when I saw him come up into the dock, even
though I was bracing myself against the shock. But to
actually see our Chris charged with murder at the Old
Bailey . . . I was only thankful no one knew who I was.'

'I'm sure. But I'm glad you went, Frank.'

'I'm glad too. At least he could see we hadn't deserted
him, however badly he's treated us.'

'Did he look pleased when he spotted you in court?'

'I don't know whether he ever did spot me. I was tucked
away at the back.' He shook his head disbelievingly as he
went on, 'But it was the way he just sat there, looking bored

and unconcerned. And him charged with murdering an old man.'

'I'm still sure he never did it.'

'It's not a pleasant thing to say of one's only son, but I believe he did.'

'No, Frank! You mustn't talk like that. Chris couldn't kill anyone. Not deliberately.'

'You weren't in court, Gwen. You didn't hear prosecuting counsel. He thinks Chris did it all right. He told the jury so.'

'That's what he's paid to say.'

'Well, if he didn't do it, why hasn't he told us he's innocent? He must know how we're feeling. When we went to see him in Brixton, we gave him the opportunity of telling us what had happened, of explaining it was all a mistake his having been arrested. But he said nothing. And after spending this morning in court, I believe he said nothing because there was nothing he could say.'

'I still shan't believe Chris did it, even if the jury convict him,' Mrs Laker declared, shaking her head as though to dispel any doubts which might be lingering there.

Her husband gazed at her in silence for several seconds. Then turning away, he said stiffly, 'Well, we've done all we could.'

It had been in the afternoon of that first day, after his father's departure, when Peter Dimitriu had gone into the witness-box and Chris found his interest in the proceedings suddenly quickening.

It was the first time he had set eyes on the son of his alleged victim, though he had, of course, been served with a copy of his evidence. He looked about thirty-five years old, was tall and thin with a slight hunch of the shoulders, and had lank fair hair and a pale pointed face whose nose gave the impression of being a natural progression of his other features. His eyes were nondescript, just functional orbs with no pretence at enhancing his overall appearance which was one of extreme watchfulness.

He took the oath in a quiet voice which had a surprisingly attractive timbre, belied by his expression. Chris had expected his voice to be high-pitched and generally grating on the ear.

As soon as he had handed the testament back to the

usher, he folded his arms across his chest and cast a quick look at where his mother was sitting like a still, black bird of ill omen. There was something intimidating about the fierce intensity of her expression. This was a woman of unyielding strength of character. A tribal matriarch.

'Is your name Peter Dimitriu?' Mr Sherway asked, in a voice which was friendly without being unctuous.

'Yes.'

'And do you live with your mother at Barnet?'

'Yes.'

'And did your father live there too until his death?'

'He did.'

'How would you describe your family life together?'

'Very happy.'

'You all got on well together?'

'Very much so. Otherwise I wouldn't have continued to live at home.'

'I haven't yet asked you, Mr Dimitriu, but what is your job?'

'I'm a freelance journalist.'

Mr Sherway's succeeding questions elicited the details of Gheorge Dimitriu's background which he had outlined in his opening speech. This done, he went on:

'Coming now to the evening of 27th February. Were you at home when your father arrived back?'

'I was.'

'And your mother was also in the house?'

'Yes.'

'Anyone else?'

'No. We have a married couple who live in, but they didn't get back from an afternoon off until just after eight.'

'And what time did your father return?'

'A few minutes before seven o'clock.'

'How long did he remain in the house?'

'Roughly forty-five minutes.'

'When he left again, did he say where he was going?'

'No, he did not.'

'Did he give any indication at all?'

'None whatsoever.'

Mr Sherway appeared to be on the verge of pursuing this line of questions when he had second thoughts.

'He left in his car?'

'Yes.'

'Alone?'

'Yes.'

'At near enough what time?'

'A quarter to eight.'

'Did you ever see him again?'

'Alive, no.'

'But you later identified his body to the police?'

'Yes.'

Mr Sherway pursed his lips and turned over a page of his notebook, only to turn it back again.

'Tell me, Mr Dimitriu, have you ever seen the accused before?'

The witness glanced unemotionally across at Chris before replying.

'No, never.'

'Did your father ever mention the accused's name in your hearing?'

'No.'

'When was the first occasion you did hear the name Christopher Laker?'

'When he was arrested. Or rather, I think it was probably a day or so before that. The police asked me if I knew him and I told them I didn't.'

'I don't think there's any dispute about this,' Mr Sherway went on, looking in the direction of Chris' counsel, 'so perhaps I may ask you what is not strictly admissable. Does the same thing go for your mother?'

'That's so. Neither of us have ever met the accused nor had we ever heard my father refer to his name.'

'Thank you, Mr Dimitriu, that's all I want to ask you.'

Mr Sherway sat down and the witness refolded his arms the other way as he watched Charles Lynn rise to cross-examine.

'Mr Dimitriu, as I understand your evidence, the accused, so far as you're concerned, never existed until after your father's death. Is that right?'

'I'm not sure that I follow the import of your question.'

Charles Lynn smiled indulgently. 'There's no import to follow, Mr Dimitriu. It's a straightforward question. You had never heard of the accused before your father's death?'

'That is so,' he replied with a puzzled air.

17

'Please don't think I'm trying to catch you out. It's simply that I want to establish certain matters beyond dispute. Did your father often go out in the evening without disclosing where he was going?'

'No.'

'You mean, he usually did say?'

'Usually, yes.'

'But not always?'

'I'm afraid I didn't keep count,' Dimitriu said sarcastically.

'On this occasion, that is the night of 27th February,' counsel continued without apparent concern, 'were you surprised when he left without a word?'

'A bit, perhaps.'

'Just a bit?'

'Yes.'

'Did you or your mother ask him where he was going?'

'No.'

'Or when he'd be back?'

'No.'

'Why was that?'

'Because it wasn't all that unusual. He sometimes had evening business appointments which he had to go to.'

'And you assumed that this was one of those occasions?'

'Yes.'

'Would it be fair to describe your father as a secretive man, Mr Dimitriu?'

The witness bit tentatively at his lower lip before replying. 'He certainly didn't discuss all his business affairs at home, if that's what you mean.'

'He had very wide business interests, I believe?'

'Yes.'

'And was a wealthy man?'

'Yes.'

'One may assume therefore that he was an astute businessman?'

'I don't think there's any doubt about that. His whole life reflects it.'

'Did he make many enemies?'

'Certainly not.'

'Why so certain? After all, it's not unknown for successful businessmen to acquire enemies in the course of achieving their success.'

Dimitriu gave a vexed frown. 'So far as I'm aware,' he said, 'my father didn't have any enemies. Not enemies in the sense you mean. People who wanted to kill him.'

Charles Lynn gazed at him with a bland expression. 'Don't be cross with me, Mr Dimitriu. You've told us that your father didn't often talk about his business affairs at home. From that, may I take it that you were not personally acquainted with his business associates?'

'No. Apart from one or two.'

'Quite so. And those you did meet were men from the same station of life as your father?'

'I suppose so. I didn't give it much thought.'

'What I was getting at was this. None of those you ever met were unemployed young men in their twenties?' When the witness didn't answer, he pressed, 'Well, were they?'

'No. Not the ones I met.'

'Were you surprised to learn from the police that your father had allegedly been having dealings with the accused? Or, at any rate, they knew one another?'

'Not particularly.'

'But why not?'

'Because I've already explained that he wasn't given to discussing his business affairs at home. I don't pretend to know whom he met, or didn't meet, in the course of his work.'

'I'm much obliged, Mr Dimitriu,' Charles Lynn said urbanely, 'that's very fairly put. I now want to ask you a few questions on a slightly delicate matter and I apologise in advance for intruding on something as personal. You have told us that your father was a highly successful businessman who made a lot of money. Exactly how much did he leave?'

'The estate is still being wound up. A final figure hasn't been arrived at.'

'No, but give me a rough figure?'

'I can't, because a lot of his assets are still the subject of valuation.'

'Well, let me ask you this, then. Does it appear that the value of his estate is going to be considerably less than expected?'

'Expected by whom?' the judge inquired, looking up

from his note-taking like a zebra startled at a water-hole.

'By his family, my lord. Is that not so, Mr Dimitriu?'

'I gather it may be less.'

'Considerably less?'

Mr Justice Legat laid down his pen and fixed Chris' counsel with a hard look. 'I'm not sure that I follow the purpose of these questions, Mr Lynn, or their relevance to the issues with which the jury are concerned. Does it matter whether the deceased died a rich man, or a less rich man than the world had been led to believe? That is not an altogether uncommon state of affairs these days. Supposing his estate *was* less substantial than his family expected, how does that assist us in this court?'

'I apologise, my lord, if I've been trespassing on your and the jury's time by pursuing irrelevancies, but what I was seeking to establish was that the deceased was a secretive man where his business affairs were concerned and that there was an additional mystery concerning the size of his estate.'

'I'm not sure that you have proved anything which could be termed a "mystery", but even if you had, where does it take you?'

'It tends to show that the deceased's life was not the sort to have brought him into contact with my client. That they had nothing in common at any point, but that on the other hand it was a life in which he may well have made powerful enemies.'

'It seems,' the judge remarked dryly, 'that you have contrived to give the evidence yourself, Mr Lynn. However, I don't consider it to be a matter for further pursuit and, subject to anything which transpires later, I shall, when the proper time comes, advise the jury that it is not an issue which need greatly concern them.

'Now, do you have any further questions you wish to ask this witness?'

'Very few, my lord,' Lynn said urbanely and turned back to the witness. 'Do you know Mr Reyman, Mr Alex Reyman?'

'Yes. He was my father's partner in a large number of business deals.'

'Was he also a personal friend of your family?'

'He and his wife used to visit my parents for dinner and

vice versa, if that's what you mean.'

'Did he and your father get on well?'

'I can't answer that. You must ask Mr Reyman.'

'And I take it, he would know much more about your father's business associates than you do?'

'Most certainly.'

'That's all I want to ask this witness, my lord.'

As Lynn sat down, Mr Sherway indicated that he didn't wish to re-examine and Peter Dimitriu vacated the witness-box.

Chris watched him go and sit next to his mother. He whispered something in her ear and inclined his head to catch her answer. Meanwhile, the next witness, Alex Reyman, had come into court. Chris decided that he resembled a night-club bouncer. He was about six feet tall and proportionately broad. He had black, well-oiled, curly hair, a nose that looked as if it had been broken a dozen times or more, and a massive chin with a deep cleft in the centre.

The testament disappeared from view in his hand as he took it from the usher and he spoke the words of the oath in a voice that made them sound as if they were being filtered through thick soup.

'Has he got a heavy cold or something?' Mr Sherway whispered to his junior.

'I gather he always talks like that.'

'Poor chap!'

Quite apart from his thug-like appearance and congested sounds of speech, Mr Sherway wished he could dispense with the witness. His evidence was short and seemingly uncontroversial, and indeed, it could have been read to the court, had the defence not said they wanted his attendance in person. It was now clear to Mr Sherway why they wanted him. They were going to develop the theme of the deceased making enemies in the course of the cut and thrust of a high-powered business life. On the other hand, he couldn't help thinking that all this stress on Dimitriu having been a man of mystery was double-edged from their point of view. After all, if he was that secretive, the jury might well conclude that a mysterious assignation with Laker was as likely as not. However, the defence knew what it was about, and meanwhile he had to examine Mr Reyman, who was standing in the witness-box as though expecting cannon-balls rather than questions.

The sole purpose of his evidence, so far as the prosecution was concerned, was to prove the mileage on the clock in the deceased's Bentley ten minutes before he arrived home on the evening of his death. It had come about in this way. Mr Reyman had fetched the deceased's car from the garage at Dimitriu's request and Dimitriu had then suggested that he, the witness, should drive as far as the point where he was going to drop off. This was about three miles from where the Dimitrius lived and he remembered noticing the milometer click up ten thousand only a few hundred yards before he got out. He added with disarming candour that he always enjoyed watching all the noughts come up. Since the deceased had arrived home only about ten minutes after parting company with the witness, it followed that the unexplained mileage had been run up between his leaving home at a quarter to eight and the car being found six miles away the next morning.

This was the simple effect of Mr Reyman's evidence and despite every presentiment to the contrary, he gave it clearly and concisely.

'He may look as if he's been fashioned out of rough clay,' Mr Sherway murmured to his junior as he sat down, 'but there's a sharp mind all right somewhere behind the scenery.'

Charles Lynn, who had reached the same conclusion, had been eyeing the witness thoughtfully as the moment of cross-examination approached.

'Did Mr Dimitriu often give you a lift home?'

'No. I normally had my own car, but it happened to be in for a service that day.'

'Do you also run a Rolls-Bentley?'

'A Jaguar.'

'Was it unusual for Mr Dimitriu to suggest that you should drive his car?'

'No. I enjoy driving much more than he did, and more often than not I'd drive his car when we were out together.'

Nothing to be gained from pursuing that any further, Lynn reflected.

'How long had you known the deceased?'

'Six or seven years.'

'And you were his partner in a great number of business deals. Isn't that so?'

'Yes.'

'You were the sole directors of Dimitriu (Development) Ltd?'

'Yes, but Mr Dimitriu was also the director of a number of other companies with which I wasn't concerned. As for Dimitriu (Development) Ltd, he owned eighty-five per cent of the share capital. I had only twelve and a half per cent.'

'Did you find Mr Dimitriu an easy person to work with?'

'He was no more difficult than most successful businessmen.'

'A bit secretive at times, was he?'

'No more than one might expect.'

'Explain that, Mr Reyman?'

The witness rested his hands on the edge of the box and leaned forward a fraction.

'What I mean,' he said firmly, 'is that most businessmen hold certain cards close to their chest in the course of an involved deal. I do it myself. Mr Dimitriu did it.'

'Did you ever have reason to suspect that he was keeping things back from you?'

'Such as?'

'Things which you were entitled to know about as his partner and co-director?'

An expression as evanescent as the last flicker of a dying bonfire crossed his face. To the few who happened to catch it, however, it was sufficient to cast doubt on the answer which came from him.

'No.'

Charles Lynn noticed it, but, since it was not part of his case to suggest enmity between the witness and the deceased, he let it go. Indeed, he had no wish to alienate the formidable Mr Reyman at this or any other stage of the proceedings. His task was simply to sow seeds in the mind of the jury about the beneath-the-surface dimensions of the case with which they were dealing, in particular those pertaining to Dimitriu's business world.

'Tell me, Mr Reyman, had you ever heard of the accused before this case began?'

'Never.'

'You had never heard Mr Dimitriu mention his name?'

'No.'

'Or seen his name written anywhere in your office?'

'Written?'

'In a letter, on a piece of paper, in an engagement diary?'

'No, never.'

'I take it you knew most of Mr Dimitriu's business contacts?'

'A great many, but not all.'

'When you say "not all", you're thinking of the other companies Mr Dimitriu was associated with and you were not?'

'I *mean* that we didn't work so much in one another's shadows that we automatically knew all the other's contacts.'

'Would it be fair to say that most of Mr Dimitriu's contacts in the business world were men from his own station of business life?'

'It's natural.'

'Did he ever to your knowledge have any dealings with any young men, who were not connected with some business transaction or other?'

'Not that I know of.'

'Is the accused the sort of person you'd have expected him to know?'

The witness turned his head and stared at Chris like a prize-fighter sizing up a doubtful opponent.

'I don't know anything about the accused, so how can I answer that?'

Lynn beat a circumspect retreat. 'Did you at the time know of, or have you since found out, any transaction or deal which might have brought Mr Dimitriu into contact with the accused?'

'No, I have not.'

'Tell me, Mr Reyman, is it easy to make enemies in the world in which you and Mr Dimitriu were operating?'

'Depends what you mean by enemies, doesn't it?'

'I mean people who bear resentments and grudges as a result of the way some deal or other turns out?'

'Certainly, the world's always full of them.'

'The business world, in particular?'

'Possibly.'

'Especially in the field of speculation and quick profits?'

'I wouldn't know.'

'Don't think I'm being offensive, Mr Reyman, but wasn't Dimitriu (Development) Ltd involved in property deals?'

'Yes.'

'And doesn't an element of speculation enter those?'

'It enters a good many business transactions.'

'I'm sure it does ...'

'And as to quick profits, I can think of places where they're quicker.'

'But it's true that Mr Dimitriu was a very successful businessman?'

'Yes.'

'Often outsmarting his competitors?'

'Out *playing* them, I'd rather say.'

'If you please!'

'Outsmarting makes it sound as if he was dishonest.'

'I entirely accept your correction.' Lynn gently tapped his pencil against the palm of his other hand and appeared momentarily lost in thought. Then looking up, he asked, 'Do you know anything about Mr Dimitriu's estate?'

'No.'

'Do you not know that the assets appear to be substantially less than expected? Than you yourself expected?' he added quickly before the judge could intervene.

A stonewall expression settled over the witness's face.

'I'm neither a beneficiary under Mr Dimitriu's will nor am I an executor, so I can't help you.'

'And if the witness could,' the judge broke in, 'I shouldn't allow him to. I've already given you my views, Mr Lynn, on this line of questioning.'

Lynn gave a small bow to the judge and sat down.

'You have no further questions to ask this witness?'

'No, thank you, my lord.'

'You wish to re-examine, Mr Sherway?'

Prosecuting counsel rose slowly to his feet, apparently making up his mind as he did so.

'Mr Reyman, you have been asked a lot of questions tending to show that the deceased was a man of mystery, who was surrounded by hidden enemies as a result of his business acumen. Can you name a single person who, to your knowledge, wanted to kill Mr Dimitriu?'

'Certainly not.'

'Do you know of anyone who ever threatened him with violence as a result of some business deal?'

'No.'

'That's all I wish to put to the witness, thank you, my lord.'

'Then we'll adjourn until tomorrow morning.'

As soon as the judge had left the court, Chris was hurried down the stairs which led from the dock to the cells beneath the court. There someone brought him a cup of tea and while he was drinking it, his solicitor, Mr Wells, arrived.

'How are you feeling?'

'All right, thanks. Gets a bit boring at times.'

'Boring?'

'Yes.'

'I don't think I'd feel bored it I was being tried for murder,' Mr Wells said reprovingly.

Chris shrugged. It was on the tip of his tongue to say, 'You should give it a try some time,' but he desisted. Instead, he said, 'How do you and Mr Lynn think it's going?'

'Well, at least there've been no surprises so far. The prosecution witnesses have said no more and no less than expected and Mr Lynn has been able to open up one or two hopeful lines.'

'Fine.'

'Well, you heard him yourself,' Mr Wells said with asperity.

Chris nodded and took a drink of tea.

'I must catch Mr Lynn before he goes back to Chambers, so if there's nothing else . . . '

'Nothing I can think of.'

'By the way, Miss Holland sent you her . . . her love.'

'Thanks. Give her mine.'

Chris felt he had almost said 'regards'. Oh, well, perhaps that was all he exchanged with Mrs Wells.

When the solicitor had gone, he finished his tea and stretched out on the bench to think. The evidence of the last two witnesses had given him a certain amount *to* think about.

Mr Wells ran into Charles Lynn just as he was leaving the robing-room. Behind came his clerk with a brief tucked beneath one arm and a wedge of law books held together by a canvas strap hanging from the other.

'How is our man?' Lynn inquired amiably.

'Unconcerned as ever. Even had the effrontery to say he was bored.' Mr Wells' tone held a note of indignation.

'He certainly is a remarkable young man. There's no evidence of any mental trouble, I suppose?'

'You might think so from his attitude, but there isn't.'

'I know the Prison Medical Officer didn't find anything in his background to suggest abnormality . . . ' He gave Mr Wells a grin. 'Anyway, it's not bad to have a client who does take his trial so calmly. Usually, they're bags of neurotic fancies. The intelligent ones, that is. And there's certainly nothing wrong with Master Laker's intelligence. With luck, he should make quite a good impression on the jury.'

'Provided he doesn't adopt a couldn't-care-less attitude in the box,' Mr Wells remarked severely.

'I doubt whether he'll do that. He must obviously hope not to be convicted and he's intelligent enough to realise that a good deal is going to depend on the impression he makes.'

'He's got an awful lot to explain away,' Mr Wells said, shaking his head gloomily.

'You think he did it, then?' Lynn asked with a faint smile.

'Frankly, Mr Lynn, I do. Don't you?'

Lynn's smile broadened. 'All I'm saying is that I think he has a chance of being acquitted on the evidence.'

'But the fingerprint! that's damning!'

'Damning without any sort of explanation, yes. But he has given an explanation. It *was* his revolver, until it was stolen.'

Mr Wells made a face and Lynn went on, 'All I'm saying is that it is an explanation. It mayn't be a very plausible one. On the other hand when you couple it with the prosecution's complete failure to prove any motive or association between Dimitriu and our chap, I think the jury might well find there was a reasonable doubt, fingerprint notwithstanding.' He made to move off. 'But a great deal is going to depend on the way he gives his evidence.' Turning to his clerk, he said, 'Ready, Peter? Can I offer you a lift as far as the Temple, Mr Wells?'

'No, I'll find a taxi, thank you, Mr Lynn. See you tomorrow morning.'

At the same time as Chris' leading counsel and solicitor were discussing the case, so were Mr Sherway, the D.P.P.'s permanent representative at the Old Bailey and Detective Chief Inspector Adams, who had found himself left in charge of the investigation when his Detective Superintendent was whisked away to hold the fort in a beleaguered division on the other side of London, most of whose C.I.D. officers appeared to have succumbed to disabilities ranging from heavy catarrh to gunshot wounds in the buttock.

They were sitting round a table in one of the rooms allocated to the D.P.P. staff. The air was thick with smoke and each was suffering from that end-of-day fretfulness which is apt to beset everyone after five hours in court. A fretfulness not helped by the realisation that the working part of the day is by no means over for any of them.

'Tell me, Mr Adams,' Sherway began, 'what's all this about the dead man's estate? There's nothing about it in your report. What are the defence getting at?'

'I don't know what they're getting at, sir. The family solicitors were pretty cagey when I spoke to them soon after Dimitriu's death. They weren't willing to discuss the matter, other than to say that they would let me know if they came across anything which seemed to have a bearing on the murder. I did get in touch with them a couple more times in the course of the inquiry, but they said they'd found nothing of interest to me. Though Mr Wynstan – he was the partner I spoke to – did say that it looked as if the estate was going to be considerably smaller than expected. When I pressed him about this, he said this was only a preliminary impression and that it would be weeks and months before a final assessment could be reached. He assured me that there was nothing which indicated fraud or anything of that sort.'

'Hmm! I gather you've gone very thoroughly into the accused's financial background?'

'As you'll have seen from my report, sir,' Adams said, in a tone to imply that everything which did matter *was* in his report, 'there's not only no evidence of the accused having received any large unexplained sums of money, but no evidence of any sudden lashing out on his part.'

'No, I appreciate you've fully covered that angle. So what does it matter how much money the hapless Mr Dimitriu left? Certainly, the judge doesn't seem very impressed by that line of questioning.'

'Surely the defence are doing no more than throwing a bit of dust into the jury's eyes,' the D.P.P.'s representative observed.

'I think so, too. Charles Lynn is pretty adept at that.' He yawned expansively. 'The air in that court is worse than in an aeroplane. It's so full of purifying chemicals, it's a wonder we don't have mauve crystals coming out of our ears.'

About twenty minutes later, they began to gather up their papers. Sherway had three hours work in Chambers ahead of him and D.C.I. Adams thought he'd be lucky if he reached home before midnight. The D.P.P.'s representative, however, reckoned that another hour would see him through.

'I must say, Laker's quite a presentable-looking chap,' Sherway remarked, as he pushed back his chair.

'He's also a very cool customer,' Adams said grudgingly.

'What's your private opinion of what actually happened?'

'He did it all right. I've no doubt about that. But why ... I just don't know! I've thought up a hundred reasons and discarded them all. I'm certain there was no sex thing between them. Blackmail seemed a possible explanation at first, but there's no evidence of money passing, nor has any subject of blackmail suggested itself.' It was in a tone of disgust that he went on, 'I've beaten my knuckles on every conceivable door without success and yet I'm darned certain there was some link between the accused and his victim. Well, there must have been, and I'd dearly like to know what it was. It's hidden there somewhere! The trouble has been that a number of people, apart from the accused, haven't wanted me to discover the whole truth of the matter. I'm sure of it.'

'Family, you mean?'

'Family and that Reyman man. Even Mr Wynstan, the

solicitor, on the last occasion we spoke.'

'You're not suggesting they've actually lied about events?'

'No, not lied, but kept silent about certain things.'

'What you might call silent liars, in fact.'

'I'll say, bloody silent liars!' Adams observed with a rueful laugh. Then: 'What do you think our chances are, sir, of getting a conviction?'

Sherway shrugged. 'Not worse than evens. You have his fingerprint, his lies about the revolver and the lab evidence of the cardigan fibres against no motive and no proof of any link between him and the deceased. Like you, I think he did it, but whether the evidence is sufficient to prove our case is more problematical. A lot is going to depend on the impression he makes in the witness-box.'

III

By the morning of the third day Janey was beginning to feel like one of those people who squat, for some obsessive purpose, on the steps of the Ministry of this or that or who queue for three days for tickets to see Nureyev. From ten o'clock until about four in the afternoon, she had sat on a hard bench outside Number 1 Court, with only a break for lunch. Apart from that, the only time she moved was to go and gaze into court through the double glass doors. By standing in one particular place,-she was able to see the back of Chris' head as he sat in the dock. She longed for him to know that she was watching him, but he never looked round, and even if he had it was barely conceivable that he could have recognised her. Her face would have been no more than a white blob from where he was.

She had never known time pass so painfully slowly, and she found it quite impossible to read, or for that matter to concentrate on anything at all. Her thoughts whipped about her mind like dry leaves blown by a strong wind.

Mr Wells had suggested that she should remain at work and that he would telephone her when the prosecution closed its case. This, he said, would give her ample time to come along in readiness to give evidence. But she knew that she'd not be able to concentrate if she was in the office. In many ways it would be worse than keeping a draughty vigil outside the courtroom.

As a matter of fact, her employer had also questioned the necessity of her spending each day at court, but she had told him that Mr Wells insisted she should be there.

The second day was even worse than the first, since familiarity brought added boredom without in any way diminishing the nervous tension. She watched a succession of witnesses go in and out of court. The fingerprint officer, the pathologist, several police officers and lastly the man from the Forensic Science Laboratory. It was at the end of the day that Mr Wells told her he thought the defence would open its case on the following one.

'Though whether we'll reach your evidence tomorrow, Miss Holland, is another matter. Laker has to give evidence first and he's bound to be in the box for some while.'

'How's the case going?' she had asked him in an anxious tone.

'Much as expected,' he had replied unsatisfactorily.

'You mean Chris still has a good chance?'

'Mr Lynn is a very able counsel and he's putting up a fine defence. He's making the Crown fight every inch of the way.'

She nodded numbly. She knew there was no point in trying to get the solicitor to commit himself to a view about the outcome, and yet this, above all else, was what she yearned for him to do. But he always turned aside her anxious questions with vague platitudes; and yet she was compelled to go on asking them each time they spoke together.

That evening after she'd returned to the room in Earls Court which had been their home until Chris' arrest, she felt lower in spirit than at any time since that event. She experienced alternating moods of strong determination and black despair these days. Sometimes she felt that no effort to help him was beyond her capacity, at others she had the sensation of being sucked through a dark tunnel which had no end and from which there was no retreat. At moments like these, her mental and physical feelings were fused into one nerve-jangling maelstrom.

The whole situation would be so much easier to bear if he had taken her into his confidence. If he had explained exactly what had happened and how he had got himself into this terrible trouble. That it was all a grotesque mistake, she accepted, but, apart from telling her it would all be sorted out in the end, and that before too long, he'd said nothing.

When she was in one of her determined moods, she was able to exult in her ignorance and draw strength from it in some curious way. The very fact that she was ready to help him when, so to speak, blindfolded could only increase their trust in one another.

On this particular evening, however, she was feeling nothing but desolate. Only one person could have brought her comfort and he was several miles of rooftops away in Brixton prison.

And then suddenly, for no particular reason, the mood began to lift and she went to bed in a much fortified frame of mind. There was, after all, something splendid in the way Chris was facing his problems alone and refusing to allow others to become involved in his troubles. It was a sign of his strength and confidence. A sure indication of his innocence.

IV

For Chris, too, the second day of his trial had been infinitely tedious. The expert and the police witnesses who came into the witness-box, each to add his piece to the jigsaw puzzle which comprised the Crown's case, were incapable of holding his interest. It was all so remote and unreal, so prosaic and finicky. Also, he'd not slept well after the first day which made his enforced presence even more of an ordeal by boredom.

That night, however, he had slept better, which was as well since he might begin his evidence the next day and knew how important it was that he should feel mentally fresh. He couldn't help wondering how many accused had been convicted through a failure to do themselves justice in the witness-box. A failure which bore no particular relation to innocence or guilt. After all you didn't have to be innocent to be acquitted of a crime. The evidence against you might be so thin that the jury were minded to acquit until you went into the witness-box and through sheer ineptitude persuaded them you were guilty.

Chris was determined that this shouldn't happen in his case. It was rare for him to take any account of impressions he was likely to make, and he'd always scorned those who did, but if his life was ever to present him with an exception to the precept this was the occasion. The twelve humdrum-looking men and women sitting half-left of him had got to be persuaded that Chris Laker was not a murderer.

And the nearer the time came, the sharper grew his determination and, with it, a suddenly clearer view of all the implications of Janey's evidence. Accordingly, during the luncheon adjournment, he sent a message saying he wanted to have a word with his solicitor.

Mr Wells arrived with the air of a doctor who has had to turn out on a winter's night.

'I've been thinking about Janey's evidence,' Chris said, 'and I'd sooner she wasn't called.'

'Not called! But she supports your alibi. Moreover, under the new law, we've had to give the prosecution notice of her evidence.'

'But aren't the jury more likely to disbelieve than believe her?'

'What makes you say that? From what I've seen of Miss Holland, I would expect her to make a favourable impression in the box.'

'But the very fact that she and I have been living together and are not married, aren't the jury bound to think that she's supporting me out of love and loyalty and all that?' Quickly he added, 'Even though she is telling the truth.'

'You think the jury will automatically discount her evidence because of prejudice?'

'Isn't it possible?'

Mr Wells swallowed hard. He felt embarrassed. He'd formed a good many reservations about his client, but he'd been very struck by Janey. In his old-fashioned way, he saw her as the proverbial good woman sticking by her erring man and possibly even redeeming him by her love. He was a straightforward man from the moral point of view and he disliked duplicity and double-talk. What he wanted to do was to ask Chris point-blank whether his alibi was true or false. But this he couldn't do, not that he was likely to be told it was false. The whole defence, however, was founded on Chris's denial not merely of the act of murder but of any part in it, backed up by his alibi and this was no moment to start cross-examining his own client. That would be taking place in court soon enough.

If it was a false alibi – and Mr Wells had his own private views on the subject – then it was likely to be shown up as such and Laker would only have himself to blame, since he'd been very careful to point out to his client the pitfalls in his defence.

'It's not for me to suggest defences. Indeed, that would be most improper. You have to tell me what your defence is. All I can then do is to indicate some of the difficulties which may be encountered.'

But as he now realised, it had been Janey herself who had taken the initiative in supporting the alibi. Chris had said he couldn't remember exactly how he'd spent that evening, save that it was in the Earls Court area and had probably been in Janey's company. It had been she who'd come to his office and said that she could clearly recall the evening and that they'd been together from seven o'clock onwards, first at a pizza bar and subsequently in two public houses which she had named. She remembered it, she said, because she had spoken to a woman at one of the pubs who told her she was psychic and could see trouble in store for her.

'I'll certainly mention the matter to Counsel,' Mr Wells remarked, 'and we must be guided by what he says.'

'You do get the point, don't you?'

'Of course I get the point,' the solicitor retorted in an affronted tone, 'but it may *be* too late to have second thoughts . . . And now I must be getting back into court. It's almost time to resume.'

Half an hour later, the evidence of Mr Mendip, the laboratory witness, wound to a finish and, gathering up his notes, he scurried away like some small, purposeful rodent.

'I now call my last witness, my lord, Detective Chief Inspector Adams.'

Chris shifted his weight on to the other buttock and prepared to listen.

Very often an inherently improbable rapport grows up

between the officer in charge of a case and the accused. Particularly where the accused is what the police think of as co-operative. But Chris had not been co-operative. He'd admitted nothing and, apart from an absence of physical resistance, had shown himself to be as hostile towards the investigation as any suspect could be.

In these circumstances, he had to expect that D.C.I. Adams wouldn't hesitate to put the boot in if presented with the opportunity.

Of rapport there'd certainly been none.

Under Mr Sherway's questioning, Chief Inspector Adams described the scene of the crime as he'd found it at 10.45 a.m. on the 28th February. From there, the questions led him to his first interview with Chris and though his voice remained dispassionate it was clear to anyone with an ear for nuance that he regarded the accused as one of the young lay-abouts of the pop era whose usefulness to society was in inverse ratio to their nuisance value to the representatives of law and order.

However, his evidence was largely uncontroversial and Mr Sherway kept him on a tight rein, so that by the time Charles Lynn got up to cross-examine he'd had little chance of digressing from the narrow path of strict fact.

'It's true, is it not, Mr Adams,' Lynn began, 'that the police have been unable to establish any motive for the murder?'

'We haven't exactly looked for one, sir.'

'Not?' Counsel's tone was mildly sardonic.

'No, sir,' Adams replied stolidly.

'Well, even if you haven't looked for one, is it fair to say that no motive has thrust itself under your nose?'

'That's correct, sir.'

'And indeed, despite very considerable efforts on your part, you have been quite unable to discover any direct link between the accused and the deceased?'

'There was the fingerprint, sir. Also the fibres from the accused's cardigan found in the car.' Adams' tone carried a note of indignation that defence counsel could attempt to overlook such telling evidence.

'Yes, I know all about the fingerprint and the fibres,' Lynn said patiently, 'but, leaving those aside for the moment, you have found no evidence at all, have you, to show that the accused and deceased ever met one another or ever had anything to do with one another? That is so, isn't it?'

'There's evidence that the accused was in the deceased's car on the night of the murder,' Adams retorted.

'You're back on the fingerprint and the fibres,' Lynn said, shaking his head sorrowfully as the witness stared at him with wooden determination. 'Let me repeat my question. There is no evidence, is there, that the accused knew Mr Dimitriu?'

'There's an overwhelming inference . . . '

'Ah yes, Chief Inspector, but inferences are not for you as a witness of fact. They're for the jury.'

'I'm well aware of that, sir.'

'Then answer my question!'

'Will you please repeat it.'

'Certainly. You have discovered no evidence that the accused was personally acquainted with the deceased?'

'Put like that, the answer is no, sir, I haven't.'

'Thank you, Chief Inspector, I don't know why you couldn't have answered it the first time.'

'Don't sermonise, Mr Lynn,' the judge said with the flicker of a smile.

'I'm sorry, my lord. I'm afraid I was thinking aloud more than sermonising.'

'One is dangerous and the other is impermissible, so now let's get on, shall we?'

Charles Lynn nodded his head in acknowledgement of the reproof.

'You have told the court, Mr Adams,' he went on, once more facing the witness, 'that you went to the accused's address as a result of information?'

'Yes, sir.'

'What information?'

'A telephone call.'

'Was it an anonymous telephone call?'

'Yes.'

'Has any effort been made to find out where it came from?'

'Yes, sir.'

'What?'

36

'We've asked for the person to come forward. Our appeal appeared in the press.'

'But no one responded?'

'I'm afraid not.'

'Was any effort made to trace the call at the time?'

'It wasn't possible.'

'Why not?'

'It was a call made to the Information Room at Scotland Yard and the caller rang off immediately he'd passed his message. I didn't receive it myself till later in the day.'

'Is it usual to act on anonymous calls in such circumstances?'

'Certainly. One follows up every lead possible in an investigation such as this.'

'What exactly did the message say?'

'It said, "A young man living in the top-floor flat at 36 Forton Street, Earls Court, may be able to help you over the murder of Mr Dimitriu." '

'It didn't mention the accused's name?'

'No, sir.'

'I imagine you would like to know, Chief Inspector, who originated that message?'

'Yes, I would, sir.'

'Because it might have been the murderer himself, mightn't it?'

The question brought Mr Sherway to his feet.

'I don't think my learned friend should ask questions which invite speculative answers of that nature.'

'Don't answer that question, Chief Inspector Adams,' the judge said.

'If you please,' Mr Lynn observed in a tone of forensic smoothness. 'Let me ask you this instead. Have you asked all the witnesses connected with the case whether they could help you over who made the call?'

'Yes.'

'But none of them could?'

'None could.'

'I should have asked you this before. Was the anonymous caller male or female?'

'Male, sir.'

It was at this point that anyone, who cared to glace at Chris, would have noticed that he appeared to be lost in frowning concentration. The truth was that he, too, was baffled by the call which had led to his interrogation and arrest. Moreover, it wasn't the only thing which was baffling him.

Lynn had meanwhile begun to question the witness about the deceased's estate, but he elicited no more than he had from earlier witnesses. He wasn't sure whether this was wholly because Chief Inspector Adams knew no more or because he had forfeited the witness' good-will when it came to answering questions in the wider field. At all events, he soon gave up and sat down.

The judge glanced at the clock and then at defending counsel.

'We have about a quarter of an hour left, Mr Lynn. I'm ready to adjourn early if you wish. On the other hand, I'm prepared to continue if that is convenient to you.'

'I'm most grateful to your lordship, but I don't propose to open the defence to the jury, so I'll be calling my client straightaway. In those circumstances, your lordship may consider it would be better for everyone if we began fresh with his evidence tomorrow morning.'

'So be it.'

Outside court, Mr Wells buttonholed Charles Lynn and put to him Chris' anxiety about Janey's evidence. Counsel listened with head cocked on one side and then made a face.

'She's perfectly willing to give evidence, isn't she?' he asked when the solicitor had finished.

'More than willing. She's most anxious to do so.'

'Of course, if the jury thinks she's being quixotically loyal, it'll be too bad. But that's a standard risk with alibi witnesses: they're invariably mums or wives or girl-friends.'

'That's Laker's point.'

'Well, let's see how his evidence goes and decide then. Though at the moment my feeling is that we ought to call her. We've served notice of her evidence and, though no one can comment on her absence if we don't call her, one can never be sure what mayn't slip out.' He made to move towards the robing-room. 'I confess that I've never yet come across an alibi that didn't smack of contrivance. Even when they're genuine, they manage to have a spurious air. Like tarts with hearts of gold.'

38

v

When Chris stepped into the dock at exactly one minute after half past ten the next morning, he was immediately aware that all eyes were turned towards him. The twelve jurors studied him with the impassivity of a group of cows watching the approach of a stranger.

Mrs Dimitriu, seemingly more enveloped in swathes of black than ever, stared at him with eyes which sought to bore into the deeper recesses of his mind. The moment was near, she clearly thought, when the enigma of her husband's death was to be explained.

Even the judge was looking at him with an air of steely appraisal during those few seconds while the court settled before Charles Lynn rose and said simply, 'I call my client.'

For the first time since his trial began, Chris moved outside the confines of the dock. One of the prison officers unlatched the door and Chris stepped through and made his way to the witness-box, aware that everyone's gaze followed him, watching intently for omens. The guilty always tripped or hung their heads: the innocent looked neither to left nor right and scratched at some part of their anatomy. Or vice versa. Where omens were concerned, you took your choice.

Chris took the oath in a nicely calculated tone, intended the convey a belief in simple truth and a quiet confidence in the English legal system. He had rehearsed this in the prison latrines until he felt that Sir Laurence Olivier couldn't have given a better performance.

Even Mr Wells was impressed and wondered whether some of his judgements on his client might not have been a little harsh.

Mr Sherway, however, whispered dryly to his junior, 'He's not only a murderer, but an actor, too!'

In the brief silence which followed his taking of the oath, Chris decided that it would look better to stand with his hands clasped behind his back, rather than rest them on the ledge of the box in front of him. It was more dignified, less confidently informal. Even as the thought came to his mind, he realised, not without an element of self-disgust, how far he was prepared to conceal his true feelings about his trial. He was like someone taking part in a hated game of charades with maximum good grace.

He now looked over the heads of those sitting in the well of the court at his counsel who was standing looking back at him with his head slightly on one side. Then glancing down at the papers in front of him, Lynn began his questions. The preliminary formal ones were asked in a voice which appeared to reflect a complete lack of interest in the answers. But these over, he looked up sharply and in a very clear voice said:

'Did you murder Gheorge Dimitriu?'

'No, sir.'

'Did you know him at all?'

'No, I did not.'

'So far as you aware, had you ever met him or heard of him?'

'No.'

Thereafter, he took Chris quite briefly through his evidence. His movements on the night of the murder as far as he could recall them, the apparent theft of the murder weapon from his room, the fact that the cardigan from which the significant fibres came had been bought in a multiple store which sold them by the thousand, the sudden panic which had caused him to lie to Detective Chief Inspector Adams about the revolver.

The questions were skilfully framed to elicit in as undamaging a way as possible the more damning parts of Chris' evidence. No time was wasted in dwelling on its more dubious aspects and he was careful not to give Chris any licence to expand at his peril on what was better left unexpanded. In just under half an hour he sat down, his examination-in-chief completed.

Mr Sherway rose to cross-examine with the air of a bridge player, undecided about his opening bid. Chris licked his lips and waited. Answering his own counsel's questions had been one thing, but facing the man who was about to subject him to verbal surgery was another. In the few seconds while he waited for prosecuting counsel's first question, he felt tenser than he ever had before. Worse than tense, apprehensive to the point of near panic. He bit nervously at the corner of his mouth. If only he had some idea of what that first question was going to do. A rivulet of sweat began to run between his shoulder blades and he gave a small wriggle to try and halt its downward progress by contact with his shirt.

And then the question came, asked in a quiet conversational tone. Except that it wasn't the sort of question normally asked in quiet conversation.

'Are you a very selfish person, Mr Laker?'

Chris blinked owlishly. It was the last sort of question he'd expected. A foolish grin almost formed on his face out of sheer relief, but he checked it in time. God, he'd have to watch out. He couldn't let his reactions get out of control at this juncture.

'I don't think I'm more selfish than the average person,' he replied in a nicely judged tone of self-deprecation.

'Not?' Mr Sherway observed mildly. 'Then let us examine the question in a little more detail. You have no regular job, do you?'

'That's true.'

'You only work when economic necessity dictates, isn't that so?'

'Yes, that's more or less true.'

'And for as short a time as possible?'

'I suppose so.'

'Don't *suppose*, Mr Laker; but isn't it a fact that as soon as you have earned sufficient money to tide you along you give up whatever job it happens to be?'

'That's certainly been the case on a number of occasions.'

'Would it be fair to say that when you work you do so for the maximum amount of money in the shortest possible time?'

'Yes, within reason.'

'What do you mean by "within reason"?'

'Well, sometimes I haven't taken the best-paid job. I've gone for another.'

'Why was that?'

'Because it was a pleasanter job.'

'On such occasions as you mention, was there all that much difference in pay between the two jobs?'

'I can't remember specific details.'

'Is that because you've had so many jobs?'

Chris blinked again. It seemed a good tactic when the

heat became uncomfortable. It was certainly better than allowing yourself to be stung into answering back. And one or two of prosecuting counsel's questions had stung.

'No, it's because I've never kept any record of what I've been paid at various jobs.'

'I don't wish to spend too much time pursuing this particular matter, Mr Laker, but would it be fair to sum up your attitude as a search for easy money rather than for a job in which to fulfil yourself?'

'I've often had to work very hard for my money. I wouldn't call it easy money.'

'But when you've been on the lookout for a job, your prime interest has been maximum return for minimum effort. That's true, isn't it?'

'I've never done anything dishonest, if that's what you mean,' Chris replied firmly.

But Mr Sherway's mind was already forging down another track.

'This revolver you bought off a workmate, what did you want it for?'

'I didn't really want it. But I've always been mildly interested in firearms and he wanted to get rid of it and well . . , I bought it.'

'But why?'

'I've just explained.'

'You bought it because of your interest in firearms?'

'Yes.'

'Did it occur to you to obtain a firearms certificate for it?'

'Yes.'

'But you didn't?'

'No, because I realised it wouldn't sound very good if I said I'd bought it from a workmate, whose name I didn't know.'

'And that was the only reason?'

'Yes.'

'Why didn't you tell Detective Chief Inspector Adams the truth when you were first asked if you owned a revolver?'

'Because I was frightened.'

'Frightened of what?'

'The very fact the question was asked indicated that the police knew something. After all, sir,' Chris went on, glad of the opportunity of turning the question, 'if I had known that my revolver had been used to murder Mr Dimitriu and was actually in the possession of the police at that moment, I'd hardly have been so foolish as to deny ownership. I did deny it, but out of panic. I didn't even know it had been stolen then.'

'Do you often get into panics?'

'No, but being questioned by the police can be disconcerting. Particularly since it was obvious they suspected me of something. It was only after that first interview that I discovered the revolver was missing from the drawer in which I kept it.'

'When had you last seen it?'

'About two weeks before.'

'Did you either then or subsequently discover that anything else had been stolen?'

'No.'

'Only the revolver?'

'Yes.'

'Does that strike you as remarkable?'

'No, because there wasn't anything worth stealing.'

'No money?'

'I always carried my money on me. We never left anything valuable in the flat for the reason that it wasn't very secure.'

'So what you're telling the jury is that on some unknown day a mysterious intruder entered the flat, stole the revolver and made off without your ever being aware of what happened?'

'It must have been like that.'

Mr Sherway left the subject of the revolver and Chris took the opportunity of reclasping his hands the other way round behind his back. He felt he had emerged fairly creditably from that aspect of their encounter.

Prosecuting counsel now turned to testing his denial of any sort of relationship with the deceased. After half a dozen questions, it was apparent to Chris that Mr Sherway had no surprise to spring and his confidence increased. On the other hand, he was careful not to appear either complacent or stroppy.

Mr Lynn, who had been intently observing his client's performance under cross-examination, bent forward and

whispered to Mr Wells who was sitting immediately in front
of him.

'He's an extremely good witness.'

'Not too good, I hope,' Mr Wells hissed back.

'I think the jury are impressed.'

'Have you decided whether to call the girl?'

'I think we will.'

It was another ten minutes before Mr Sherway completed his cross-examination and sat down. Mr Lynn asked
only four questions in re-examination and Chris was about
to turn and leave the witness-box when the judge spoke.

'I have one or two questions to ask,' he said, in a tone a
boa-constrictor might use in addressing its next meal.

Chris stared at the red-robed figure on the bench in
surprise. Mr Justice Legat had asked very few questions
and it had somehow not occurred to Chris that he might
come in for any.

The judge had a curious habit of twitching his lips as a
preliminary to actual speech, and Chris now found himself
mesmerised by this as he stood waiting.

'You have told the jury that you acquired this revolver
because of your mild interest in firearms,' he began, giving
the word 'mild' a rather suggestive inflexion; 'that is so, is it
not?'

'Yes, sir.'

'That you had no particular use for it, but bought it from
this unknown workmate who wanted to get rid of it. That
was what you said, wasn't it?' This time it was 'unknown'
which received the benefit of his gift for innuendo.

'That's correct, sir.'

The judge nodded in a satisfied way. 'Perhaps, then, you
would tell the jury why you thought it necessary to acquire
ammunition for it.'

'It was part of the deal. I didn't buy the ammunition
separately, sir. This chap was offering the revolver and
ammunition together.'

'All right, but was there anything to prevent your throwing away the ammunition afterwards?'

'I suppose not.'

'Why didn't you?'

'It didn't occur to me.'

'But you've told the jury you had no intention of using

the revolver, so wouldn't it have been better to have destroyed the ammunition?'

'I suppose it would.'

'But you didn't?'

'No, sir.'

'In fact, you kept both revolver and ammunition together in the same drawer?'

'Yes.'

'Now tell me something else. How often did you take the revolver from its place of keeping and examine it?'

'Once or twice a week perhaps. I didn't have any regular time for doing so.'

'And you'd take it out and play with it?'

'Yes. I suppose you'd call it playing.'

'And that was all you ever intended doing with it?'

'Yes.'

'And finally, it wasn't until the police spoke to you that you discovered it was missing?'

'That's correct, sir.'

'That means you hadn't had occasion to take it out and play with it for at least ten 'days?' This time there was a nastly little bit of emphasis on 'play'.

'That's so, sir.'

'Very well, you may go back to the dock; unless, Mr Lynn,' he added turning to defending counsel, 'you have anything you wish to ask your client arising out of my questions?'

'No thank you, my lord.'

'Very well.' He waved an arm of dismissal in Chris' direction.

When Chris returned to the dock, he didn't even notice the harsh discomfort of his chair. It was all he could do to stop himself shaking like a vibrator. He felt as if he'd been running across a softly ploughed field which had no end. More than anything else he wanted to cast his mind back over his evidence and form some critical judgement of the impression it had made. But he found this impossible. He couldn't see it as a whole, only in a hideously distorted perspective.

He took off his spectacles and rubbed his eyes. God, he felt whacked. He'd never had such an experience before. His unreal sense of detachment had been transformed into a feeling of being a pulp of mangled components.

It was some time before he realised that Janey was in the witness-box. She had just taken the oath and was darting her eyes from Mr Lynn to himself.

Janey! He hadn't seen her since the trial began and there she was! He was too exhausted to entertain his earlier worries about the effect of her evidence. As he looked up, she smiled at him shyly and he smiled back. It was meant to be a reassuring smile, not that he felt in any condition to reassure anyone.

Then Mr Lynn's questions began and she gave him all her attention. Chris watched her, filled with growing gratitude. Gone, temporarily, at least, was his fear of being put under obligation to her. At this moment he could feel only thankful for her friendly presence in court. God knows how the future would turn out, but he determined that he would always try and remember this moment.

Standing in the witness-box, she looked small and vulnerable. She was wearing a dark blue frock which had a broad cape-like collar of burgundy red and cuffs of the same colour. Her hair, which was dark brown, just reached to her shoulders and had a tendency to fall forward to mask the left side of her face. She never used much make-up, but it looked to Chris as though she had on none. Perhaps Mr Wells had dropped one of his hints.

Chris forced himself to listen to her evidence.

'What makes you remember the evening of 27th February so clearly, Miss Holland?' Lynn was asking.

'It was the evening I spoke to this woman in the Yardarm Public House who told me she had psychic powers and could see a lot of trouble in store for me. I'm not superstitious, but there was something about the way she said it. It stuck in my mind.'

'You'd never met this woman before?'

'No.'

'Or seen her since?'

'No.'

'And Mr Laker was with you the whole of that evening?'

'Yes. From the time I got back from work just after six until we went to bed.'

'He was never out of your company long enough to make

46

a journey to Barnet and back?' Lynn asked with a faint smile.

'Definitely not.'

'Thank you, Miss Holland.'

Mr Sherway rose with his usual thoughtful air.

'How long have you known the accused, Miss Holland?'

'Fifteen months exactly.'

'And you're very fond of him?'

'Yes.'

'Deeply in love with him, in fact?'

'Yes.'

'You'd do anything to help him?'

'I'd do a lot, yes.'

'Where would you stop short?'

'I don't know.'

'Would you lie to help him?'

'I might do.'

'In the witness-box?'

Janey flushed. 'My evidence is the truth.'

'What makes you remember the evening of 27th February so clearly?' Mr Sherway asked, his point made.

'I've already explained that.'

'Yes, but why do you associate your conversation with this psychic lady with that particular evening? Couldn't it just as well have taken place on 26th February or the 28th or the 23rd?'

'I just do remember it.'

'But you must have had some reason. I mean, you didn't immediately look at a calendar after this curious conversation and say to yourself "it's 27th February", did you?'

'No, of course not.'

'Then, what makes you associate this conversation with that date? That's all I'm trying to find out from you, Miss Holland.'

'Well, I mean, why does one remember a whole lot of things?'

'You're there to answer counsel's questions, Miss Holland, not the other way about,' the judge said with a telling sniff.

Janey cast him a look of distaste. She disliked being pushed around and though she'd never been inside a court before and had felt slightly overawed at the start, she'd

47

found herself becoming increasingly irritated by Mr Sherway's persistent questions.

'In the first place I remember it was a Thursday,' she said wearily. 'And I know it wasn't the previous Thursday because that was an evening I stayed late in the office to type a manuscript. And it certainly wasn't the Thursday after the 27th as I had two days off with a very heavy cold at the end of that week. So it must have been Thursday, the 27th.'

'You've worked it all out, haven't you, Miss Holland?' Sherway said in a gently reproving tone.

'I don't know what you mean.'

'Never mind; I'm sure the jury do.'

Lynn jumped to his feet. 'My learned friend really must refrain from making prejudicial comments of that nature. It's most improper.'

'I agree, I shouldn't have done so,' Sherway said sweetly. 'I apologise, my lord.' He turned back to Janey. 'Tell me, Miss Holland, how many evenings a week do you and the defendant spend in each other's company? Or I should say, how many *did* you at that period?'

'Most.'

'Except when you stayed late at the office?'

'That's only rarely, for some special reason.'

'Did the defendant ever go out on his own without you?'

Janey hesitated a second, then said in an over-casual tone, 'Occasionally.'

'Where would he go?'

'I don't know. I didn't ask him, it was none of my business.' She looked suddenly cross and flustered and gazed down at her feet.

'You mean he'd go out without telling you where he was going?' Sherway pressed.

'Yes, occasionally,' she replied, looking up defiantly.

'And you never asked him where he was going or where he'd been?'

'No. He'd have told me if he'd wanted me to know.'

Mr Lynn and Mr Wells exchanged a meaningful glance and Chris himself stared woodenly ahead. Janey's loyalty was leading her into a perilous maze, of the presence of which she seemed wholly unaware.

'How long would he be away on these occasions?'

'Just the evening.'

'Three or four hours?'

'I didn't use a time-keeper,' she retorted sharply, 'so I can't tell you.'

Mr Sherway bent over and whispered to his junior, 'Do you think I can take this any further?'

'No, I'd leave it. It obviously riled her like hell when he did go off without a word, but if you press it, she may start covering up. You've cast sufficient doubt on her reliability as an independent witness of truth.'

Sherway nodded and straightened up. 'I've no further questions, my lord.'

Mr Lynn rose to re-examine. This was a moment for trying to show that an extremely astute piece of cross-examination had been no more than the attention of a tiresome but harmless gnat. With an air of massive confidence he said, 'Just tell me this, Miss Holland, have you the slightest doubt in your own mind that Thursday, 27th February, was the evening you spent in the defendant's company at the café and two public houses you have mentioned?'

'None whatsoever,' Janey replied gratefully.

'Thank you, Miss Holland, that's all. And that, my lord, is the defence case.'

Janey left the witness-box and picked her way to a seat somewhere at the back, stared at by the Dimitrius and Reyman. Mrs Dimitriu turned and said something to her son, who frowned and shook his head.

Chris, whose thoughts had danced off elsewhere, became aware that his counsel was addressing the jury. He realised with a shock that the trial was rapidly approaching its end. Two speeches and a summing-up and then only the verdict to come.

Tomorrow it would all be over. He'd either be ... But he refused to consider the alternative. He was going to be a free man. To think that he'd be making love to Janey again tomorrow night. And the night after that, and the following one ...

Nevertheless, one thing was quite certain. The end of the trial and his freedom wouldn't mark the end of the whole affair.

Others might believe they had a monopoly in the search for the truth of what had happened, but Chris also had things he wanted to find out.

He glanced across at the jury who were listening to prosecuting counsel with expressions ranging from stolid interest to glazed boredom.

They'd got to acquit him. They'd got to ...

VI

Dick Sherway was not given to impassioned advocacy, on the other hand his closing speeches were invariably models of closely reasoned and cogent argument. He never attempted to make forensic bricks without the necessary straw, but, equally, those he did make were guaranteed to withstand the more eroding effects of an average defence plea.

' . . . At times during his trial, members of the jury,' he was saying, as Chris forced himself to listen, 'my learned friend may have given you the impression that the prosecution didn't have a case. If so, it is a tribute to his skill as an advocate. But, you know, the prosecution do have a case – and you will observe that I said "do", not "did". They have a case based on hard, unshaken evidence. Let us just look at it together for a few minutes.

'That Mr Dimitriu was murdered – brutally murdered at that – there can be no doubt. And what is found at the scene of his murder, members of the jury? First, a revolver, the weapon with which he had been killed. And whose revolver is it? It's the accused. He has admitted that, but if further proof is necessary, you have a fingerprint found on the revolver which was made by him. Of course, he has given you an explanation. Whether or not it's a very satisfactory explanation is for you to say. But supposing you are inclined to say to yourselves, "Well, I suppose it *could* have been stolen without his ever becoming aware of the fact and his fingerprint *could* have remained intact all the while it was in someone else's possession and the someone else *could* have used it to commit this murder without either removing the accused's fingerprint or imparting one of his own on it . . . " Supposing you say that to yourselves – and I hope I'm not straining your credulity by suggesting that you may be doing so – then surely you look around to see what other evidence there is. And in doing that, you come across the second significant item found at the scene of the murder. Fibres! Fibres taken from the front passenger seat which are identical with those from a cardigan owned by the accused and worn by him that very day.

'A revolver and fibres which link him with the scene of the crime. The one indicates his presence in the car, the other the purpose for which he was there.

'And when eight days later, Mr Laker is interviewed by the police, what is his first immediate reaction? To tell lies, members of the jury. He has told you that he panicked.' Mr Sherway • paused and appeared to weigh this possibility. 'Well, you have heard him give evidence, you have observed him while he did so. You will also have been observing him as he sat in the dock. Has he struck you as the sort of young man who would panic easily?'

It was clear what prosecuting counsel thought the answer to that should be. Moreover, it was a question which caused four members of the jury to turn and gaze at Chris, who decided to meet the situation by bowing his head and staring at the floor between his feet. He didn't like being examined with such interest. It was embarrassing, as well as forcing one into artificial attitudes.

' . . . Finally, members of the jury, let us consider for a moment the evidence of Miss Holland, who purports to provide the accused with an alibi for the evening in question. You may have thought that Miss Holland would have been prepared to say anything which she believed would help the accused. And let me quickly add that I don't mean that cynically or unkindly. Devotion and loyalty are two very attractive qualities, but in certain circumstances they can perhaps not provide the strongest incentive to tell the truth. It is for you, as men and women of the world, to assess the value of Miss Holland's evidence. If you come to the conclusion that her heart was ruling her head and that her purported clear recollection of the evening of 27th February was not as persuasive as she was hoping to make it, then you're back once more with the question of why she has lied. That, of course, is the fatal thing about an alibi. If it doesn't stand up, everything crashes with it.'

Sherway gave a hitch to his gown and resettled his wig slightly further forward on his head.

'Members of the jury, maybe the prosecution have been unable to establish a motive for this crime; maybe they have been unable to prove any direct link between the accused and his victim, but are you left in any real doubt that the person who shot Mr Dimitriu dead on the night of 27th February is the person sitting there in the dock? Are you in any real doubt about that; having regard to the fingerprint on the revolver, the owner of the revolver, those tell-tale fibres and the lies with which the accused first met the police? If, of course, you are left in any reasonable doubt, members of the jury, you will acquit him. But are you really left in any such doubt? The prosecution suggest that you shouldn't be and that, in fact, they have discharged the burden of proof which rests upon them in every criminal trial. In this case, of proving to your satisfaction that Christopher Joyce Laker murdered Gheorge Dimitriu on the evening of 27th February.'

VII

Charles Lynn had been addressing the jury for only twenty minutes when the court adjourned for the day. Knowing that he wouldn't be able to complete his speech, he had spun out time. There was no point in developing any line of argument when the jury were going to disperse. By the morning, such impact as he might have made on them would have become stale. To repeat what he'd said would be to diminish, for some of them at least, the overall effect of his speech. Not to repeat would, for others, be akin to never having said.

When the moment of adjournment did come, the judge turned to the jury and, after giving his usual impression of chasing grape pips around his front teeth, said, 'I think I may safely predict, members of the jury, that the case will finish tomorrow at what we may hope will be a reasonable hour. At this stage, it is more important than ever that you should not discuss it with those whom you'll be meeting outside this court, nor allow yourselves to be influenced by anything you may read in your newspapers between now and our resuming tomorrow morning. Keep your minds clear of all preconceived judgements of the issues until you retire to consider your verdict.'

Then they all stood while the court usher intoned his end-of-day piece, Mr Justice Legat bestowed bows on counsel and jury and, picking up the black cap and pair of white gloves which formed part of his judicial regalia, walked slowly out of court to the accompaniment of bowing officials.

Chris watched all this impassively. From the start, he had thought the judge's arrival and departure must be one of the most sycophantic pieces of ceremonial ever devised by man. Granted the judge represented the Queen – though that in itself struck him as an idiotic fiction – but not even she gave herself such solemn airs and graces.

On the other hand, Mrs Dimitriu, who, until now, had never set foot inside a court during twenty-odd years in her adopted country, never failed to be emotionally stirred by the daily ritual which began and ended the proceedings. And as those who knew her best could testify, she was not a person whose heart was easily stirred in such directions.

'I want to speak to Inspector Adams,' she announced to her son as she was leaving the court that day. 'Go and find him.'

'He's probably busy, Mother.'

'I want to speak to him. Anyway you are wrong, Peter, I see him coming along the corridor now.' Her voice was harsh and throaty, and her English, though fluent, was quite heavily accented. 'Inspector Adams,' she called out when he came within hailing distance.

He looked across and then came over to where she was standing near the top of the main staircase.

'Good evening, Mrs Dimitriu. Still here, I see.'

'Naturally, I am still here.'

'Has the trial satisfied your curiosity about your husband's death?'

'Of course it has not.'

'I was afraid it wouldn't.' He gave a shrug. 'As you know, the police haven't found it an easy case. There're a lot of unsolved ends.'

He had no particular liking of Mrs Dimitriu and had early on discovered that a sympathetic approach was a waste of time. She neither expected nor wanted it. Revenge seemed to be her only interest in her husband's death. Adams wouldn't have put it past her to be carrying a pearl-handled stiletto somewhere beneath all her black drapes.

'What is going to happen to this Laker? she asked, watching him with the same burning expression she was constantly focusing on Chris in court.

'He ought to be convicted, but whether he will be is another matter.'

'And if he's not?'

'Then he walks out a free man.'

'And what will you do?'

'Nothing. There's nothing I can do.'

'Nothing?'

'Nothing.'

'Even though he's a murderer?'

'The jury'll have said he isn't.'

'You will keep him under observation, though?'

Adams gave a weary laugh. 'We don't have enough men to catch all the current criminals, let alone to deploy them on watching the acquitted ones.'

'So you will do nothing?'

'No. And nor must you, Mrs Dimitriu.'

'What do you mean, Inspector?'

'I know you've expressed determination to unearth the truth about your husband's death; well, no one can prevent your trying to do that, but make sure you don't step outside the law.'

She tossed her head scornfully. 'I have sworn to find out the truth of Gheorge's death and no one will stop me. No one.'

'Be careful, Mrs Dimitriu, that's all.' He turned to her son who had been standing silent throughout the exchange. 'I'm sure you will see that your mother doesn't do anything rash.'

'Of course, she won't.'

'That's fine then. Anyway, we'll hope that Laker will be convicted.'

Secretly, Adams thought that Chris might be a good deal safer if he were to be convicted. He'd be removed from where Mrs Dimitriu could get at him. Not that he believed she was really likely to try and kill him, but the mystery of her husband's death clearly obsessed her mind and he had no doubt that she would pursue him, probably by means of a trail of private detectives.

Once the case was over, whatever the result, he didn't wish it to give rise to any further violent eruptions.

Nevertheless, even though he had told Mrs Dimitriu that there was nothing he could do if Chris were acquitted, this didn't exactly reflect his intentions, for acquittal or conviction, he was as determined as she was to come nearer the truth of the matter than he had managed so far. Moreover, he thought he'd be able to make out a case to ensure the support of his superiors.

VIII

Janey arrived at court the next morning, hot, flustered, resentful and desperately apprehensive.

Hot, because she had just missed a bus and then, after waiting for another for over ten minutes, had decided she'd have to take a taxi. But all the taxis were occupied until, after half-running the length of Piccadilly, she found one disgorging its passenger and leapt in just as someone else was about to clamber in the other side. It was an elderly man who had glared at her and, after some hesitation, gone off mumbling.

Flustered and resentful for two reasons. First because she still smarted every time she thought about her performance in the witness-box and secondly because she had called in at her place of work on the way and immediately become involved in a nerve-wringing row with her employer. He had been expecting her back and was extremely cross when she announced she'd be at court another day.

'I thought you were giving your evidence yesterday,' he had said in a grating tone.

'I did.'

'Then why do you have to go back again today?'

'I don't have to, but I feel I must. *He* needs me.'

'He being the young man in the dock?' he had said nastily.

'Yes. But I really will come in tomorrow. And I really am sorry for all the inconvenience I've caused, but I'm sure you understand.'

'All I understand is that we're apparently paying you to go and hold hands with a probable murderer.'

'He is *not a murderer*,' she had replied tartly.

'I'm only going by what I read in the papers,' he had said in a tone of infuriating superiority. 'It doesn't really matter to me whether he is or not. My interest is merely in looking after my clients and getting the work done, and this week has been a diabolical wash-out in both respects. First you were only going to be away one day, then it definitely wasn't going to be more than two, then it became three and now . . . well, I've lost count.'

'That's not fair,' she had said miserably and at the same time angrily. 'And I've said I'm very sorry.'

'Indeed, you have; though, alas, that doesn't serve to even get the date typed on a single letter.' He had turned his back on her. 'Well, you'd better be going . . . I'd have got someone else in if I'd known it was going to drag on like this . . . ' And so she had left, stung by the justness of his rebuke, as by its bitterness. She liked her job, she liked her boss and she realised how difficult things had been for him while she was away. On the other hand, she felt he might have shown a little more understanding of her position.

Part of the trouble was that she'd hardly slept at all last night for worrying about the outcome of Chris' trial, and now as she paid off the taxi and gazed up at the great stone building she was seized with the sort of fear she'd only previously known in dreams when confronted by some horrible and certain death. She saw it as a vast temple to whose esoteric Gods Chris was being offered as a sacrifice.

Shaking off her morbid reflections, she hurried inside and up the marble staircase which led to the main corridor of courts. It was twenty-five minutes past ten and Number 1 Court was almost full. She glanced anxiously around for a seat. At first there didn't appear to be one and then she saw someone move up and motion her to come and sit next to him.

'You only just made it this morning,' her companion said hoarsely, at the same time giving her a small crooked smile.

'Yes, I thought I was going to be late.' He was the first person to have spoken to her agreeably this morning and she was grateful for that tiny crumb. She recognised him as Alex Reyman and knew from corridor gossip that he had been the deceased's business partner. Indeed, though this

was the first occasion they had spoken, they had sat quite
close to one another on the first day of the trial before he'd
been called into the box to give his evidence. He was not
the sort of person to pass unnoticed and Janey had made a
point of asking one of the police officers on the courtroom
door who he was.

'I heard you give evidence yesterday,' he said, 'I gather
you're Laker's girl-friend?'

'That's right.'

'No need to ask you then,' he went on with a laugh, 'what
you hope the verdict will be.'

Janey gave an embarrassed smile. 'I also happen to believe he's innocent.'

'So you should.'

She shot him a surprised glance. 'You mean you do, too?'

'Oh, I don't know that I'd go as far as that; but he's your
boy-friend and you're sticking by him and I think that's fine
and natural.'

'I don't see how they can convict him when he didn't
even know Mr Dimitriu,' Janey said, glad to have the
opportunity of asserting her views.

'There are quite a lot of people interested in that aspect,'
Reyman remarked thoughtfully. 'Two of them sitting there.'
He nodded at Mrs Dimitriu and her son two rows in front
of them. 'The old lady for one won't rest until she has
ferreted out the truth.'

Janey shivered. 'Who's the other?' she asked in a brittle
tone.

'What other?'

'You said, "The old lady for *one*." '

'Oh, I see what you mean. That was just a figure of
speech.'

But she wondered whether it really had been . . .

Just then there were three raps on the door through which
the judge made his entry and everyone stood up. Janey's
eyes, however, were fastened on the dock. She could just
see the top of Chris' head as he stood on one of the stairs
leading up from the cells, waiting for the prison officer's
signal to him to enter the dock.

She felt tears prickling her eyes. There was something
about Chris' head which always melted her. After all, she
recalled, it was that which had first attracted her to him

before he'd ever opened his mouth and said a word. It wasn't that it was a particularly unusual shape, just an inspiring shape. So many male heads seemed to be narrow or sloping or square or flat or just functional lumps to accommodate the ears, nose and eyes. But Chris' head was interesting and comforting. It sounded idiotic, she knew, but she was in love with the shape of it.

As he came up the remainder of the stairs, she tried to catch his eye and felt desolate when she failed to do so. A moment later he had sat down and Charles Lynn was resuming his closing speech.

'When we separated yesterday evening, members of the jury, I was inviting you to see just what the prosecution's case consists of. It consists, as my learned friend has said to you very clearly, of a fingerprint, of some fibres and of some untruths which Mr Laker has quite frankly admitted telling. Let us look at those elements together for a moment. First the fingerprint. There's no dispute that it's the defendant's, just as there is no dispute that the revolver on which it was found is his. He has told you that it must have been stolen from the place where he kept it and, if you accept that, then it must have been stolen by the man who did murder Mr Dimitriu.

'Members of the jury, there are many unexplained matters connected with this case. Far too many, you may think! But it doesn't require much imagination, does it, to accept that the unknown murderer stole that revolver, used it to commit his brutal crime and then made an anonymous telephone call to the police incriminating my client. Doesn't that strike you as a very likely sequence of events? It may sound all very mysterious, but is it any more mysterious than a great number of other things connected with the case? One thing which has emerged quite clearly is that Mr Dimitriu was a man of mystery. Just reflect for a moment. On the evening of his death, he left home without a word as to where he was going and kept a rendezvous with his murderer. His *unknown* murderer, because there's not one iota of evidence that my client knew, or had ever met, him. There's not even the beginnings of a suggestion that they had ever set eyes on one another. What could be more mysterious than that unexplained departure from his house and his violent death a few hours later? The defence don't have to try and provide explanations; that's the prosecution's function. But what the defence are entitled to say is, how could you even consider convicting someone of murder on evidence so thin and at the same time so opaque?

'Well, so much for the fingerprint on the revolver. Both are Mr Laker's and he has given you an acceptable explanation of what must have happened. Of course, if you're *still* inclined to believe the version of events put forward by the prosecution, you will have to ask yourselves this compelling question. Is it likely that this young man, after carefully planning a brutal murder, would leave his revolver, together with fingerprint, at the scene of the crime? Is *that* very likely, members of the jury? Is it?'

As he spoke he ran his eyes along the double row of faces in the jury box, as though posing the question to each one of them individually.

'And now let us turn to the question of the fibres. What does the evidence amount to? That three fibres were found on the passenger seat of the deceased's car which correspond with those in the weave of a cardigan owned by the defendant. And what do we know about that cardigan? That it was bought at a multiple store who sell tens of thousands of them every year, including many thousands in that particular colour. It's like trying to prove that a particular blade of grass – or three blades of grass, if you wish – came from a certain patch of lawn, when the lawn itself is several acres in size. That's not very persuasive evidence, is it, members of the jury?'

Charles Lynn shook his head as though it sorrowed him to pick such easy holes in the prosecution's case.

'And now to the third major point made against my client. The untruths he told when first confronted by the police. Were they really all that significant or sinister when you consider the circumstances? Suddenly, without warning, the police, in the form no less of a Detective Chief Inspector and a Detective Sergeant, arrive on Mr Laker's doorstep and immediately make it apparent that he is under suspicion of some serious crime or other. They ask him whether he knows a Mr Dimitriu, where he was on the evening of 27th February and whether they may search his room. Concerning all those matters he is, the defence say, completely frank. Only when he is asked whether he owns a revolver, does he sidestep the truth. And why, members of the jury? Because he hasn't a licence for it and knows that he shouldn't possess it without one. He is also further inhibited by the somewhat unorthodox circumstances of its purchase from someone whose name he doesn't know.

'All right, none of that was very sensible of him, neither its purchase nor his denial of ownership. But that doesn't brand him as a murderer. There are very few of us who act with complete wisdom all the time. What's more I venture to suggest there are even fewer who could be guaranteed to do so in the circumstances by which my client found himself suddenly confronted, namely the probing questions of two C.I.D. officers. I invite – no, members of the jury, I *demand* that each one of you asks yourself whether *you* would have reacted so very differently in similar circumstances and I venture to suggest that the fair answer will be, "No, I wouldn't have".'

Lynn glanced down at his notebook while his words continued to ring in the jury's ears. He was given to frequent changes of tone in the course of addressing a jury so that they didn't become lulled into a state of hypnotic bemusement like viewers of some TV soap-opera.

'It has been suggested from time to time in the course of this trial,' he went on in a much crisper tone, 'that because Mr Laker doesn't choose to work full time, but only when economic necessity demands, he'd be more likely to commit a murder than someone else who puts in a forty-four hour week for fifty weeks in the year . . .'

'I've never suggested any such thing,' Sherway broke in, half rising to his feet.

'In that event – and I'm grateful to my learned friend for his intervention – perhaps I've been under a false impression. Perhaps you were, too. Notwithstanding my learned friend's assurance, I should like to say this, members of the jury. Whatever you may think about my client's way of life, there is no evidence that it has ever been other than law-abiding . . .'

'Was not his possession of a revolver without a licence a breach of the law, Mr Lynn?' the judged inquired in a voice like a sudden gust of icy air.

'I am much obliged to your lordship,' Lynn replied smoothly, 'I had been about to refer to that exception,

Members of the jury, most of us probably regard ourselves as law-abiding citizens, even though we may not pay our television licence fees on the exact date or renew our driving licences when we should, or always declare everything we bring through the Customs on our way home from a summer holiday abroad.'

At least three jurors looked faintly sheepish at this point.

'But that doesn't make us criminals in our own eyes or in the eyes of most of our friends or of society at large. I ask you to view Mr Laker's possession of the revolver in that light and not as something which is half-way to branding him a murderer.

'Finally, members of the jury, I come to the question of his whereabouts on the evening of 27th February. All he has been able to say is that I was somewhere around the Earls Court area, I don't remember the exact details, but I certainly was never at Barnet. However, Miss Holland, for the reasons she has told you, has a much clearer recollection of how he and she spent that evening, and she says that it was quite impossible that he could have been anywhere near where the murder was committed. I ask you to accept her evidence and to reject the somewhat unworthy suggestion that because she and the defendant live together, she'd be automatically prepared to commit perjury on his behalf. You saw her in the witness-box and, I suggest, she gave every impression of being a truthful witness. There was surely nothing of the glib perjurer about her evidence.'

With a fresh change of tone, Charles Lynn launched into his peroration and, a few minutes later, sat down.

The judge half turned to face the jury who, for their part, inclined themselves in his direction. They gazed at him respectfully while his mouth fretted away like a rabbit's nose. After what seemed like an unconscionable time, speech came.

In all, he summed up for just under two hours. Apart from the occasional touches of acid and sarcasm, which he knew would never be reflected in the shorthand-writer's transcription of the proceedings, it was a fair summing-up. The issues were clearly placed before the jury with a great deal less judicial comment than is often the case.

Nevertheless, as Chris listened on and off he was left in no doubt that Mr Justice Legat regarded him as the sort of

young man who could well commit a murder, even if he
hadn't committed the one charged.

' . . . Members of the jury, as I have emphasised several
times in the course of my summing-up, you, and you alone,
are the judges of fact. This case involves no law apart from
the general principles applicable to every criminal trial,
which I have enunciated. It is a case of facts and, therefore,
one which falls particularly aptly within your competence.
Address your minds to those facts with all the everyday
common sense you possess and let me know whether you
find that the prosecution have proved beyond reasonable
doubt that the accused, Christopher Joyce Laker, is guilty
of the murder of Gheorge Dimitriu. If the prosecution have
failed to prove that beyond reasonable doubt, he is entitled
to be acquitted. But if, viewing the evidence as a whole, you
find the case has been proved to your satisfaction, then it is
your duty to convict . . .'

IX

'They're giving it a good old chewing-over,' said the senior
prison officer cheerfully, glancing at his watch. He was
sitting with Chris in one of the cells below the court, waiting
for the jury to come back. They had now been out for over
an hour and a half.

An hour and a half the like of which Chris had never
known. One moment, it was all he could do not to jump up
and scream, 'Let them find me guilty now, anything's better
than this ghastly waiting.' The next, he was sunk in
apathetic gloom.

'What's that mean?' Chris asked, clutching at what
might be a straw.

'Oh, you can't draw any conclusions these days. Sometimes, they're only out a few minutes and find a chap
guilty. Other times they take Lours to make up their minds
and it can still go either way.'

'Presumably it means they don't all think I'm guilty?'

'That's right, they're having a real old argy-bargy up
there. Of course, it might be there's just one juror holding
out against the rest. That happens quite a bit. But now the

judge can take a majority verdict, it doesn't matter so much.'

Chris looked at him without affection. He was the sort of man who'd shake your hand and send you to your death with a burst of detached heartiness.

'Mind you,' he went on, 'this waiting business was much worse in the old days of the death sentence. When a bloke knew he was likely to be topped if the jury convicted him, it could really play on his nerves. Though some of 'em were still as cool as cucumbers. Usedn't to turn a hair even when the old judge put on the black cap. Nowadays, life imprisonment doesn't mean anything. You're out as soon as the Home Secretary feels like it.'

He had been picking his teeth with a match-stick most of the time he'd been talking, examining the results with interest before wiping them off on the under-edge of his chair.

'How long is it before you get sent to an open prison?' Chris asked, uncertain whether he wanted to know the answer or not.

'Depends. You'll probably start off in the Scrubs. After that, it's anyone's guess.'

'If I'm convicted, I shall certainly appeal.'

'Most of 'em do. Not that it's likely to do you much good. Seemed to me the old judge gave you quite a fair run.'

'But I really do happen to be innocent,' Chris said, stung by the other's nonchalance.

'It's all the same to me whether you're innocent or guilty. If you get away with it, good luck to you. I shan't bear you any grudges. Mind you, I don't say that to these child murderers and the ones who kill innocent people in the course of a robbery, and the likes of those. If I had my way, I'd bring back the rope for them.'

Chris shook his head slowly. The man was an anachronism: a grotesque anachronism.

'Well, yours is one job I wouldn't have at any price.'

'If it comes to that, I don't think it would have you. But it's got its points. Free accommodation and a pension at the end.'

A silence fell, during which the officer went on picking

his teeth and Chris stared mindlessly at the wall a few feet in front of him.

There was a sudden clatter of footsteps outside and the door opened to reveal the other officer.

'They're coming back.'

'O.K., Laker, on your feet. You'll soon know the worst. Feeling all right, are you?'

Chris nodded. He didn't trust himself to speak. A minute later he was standing half-way up the stairs which led into the dock. He could hear the buzz of conversation in court. Then there was a call for silence and the clerk read out the names of the jurors, who answered in turn.

There followed a further agonising wait, ending with the staccato knocks on the door which signalled the judge's entry.

Chris fixed his eyes on the officer who was at the top of the stairs, waiting to motion him up. Then it came and he completed his journey.

Now he was standing in the front of the dock, his head up and his gaze anchored to the sword which hung on the wall behind the judge's head. He had decided in advance that was where he would focus his attention. He was determined not to look at a face.

'Members of the jury, are you agreed upon your verdict?'

'We are.'

'Do you find the prisoner, Christopher Joyce Laker, guilty or not guilty of murder?'

'Not guilty.'

Chris was still staring bemusedly at the sword after the judge had gone out. He became aware of someone plucking at his sleeve.

'Come on, Laker,' the familiar voice hissed. 'Don't act so surprised.'

PART II

I

Detective Chief Inspector Adams got out of his car and paused a moment on the pavement to gaze up at the brash building which was now the headquarters of the Metropolitan Police. To him, it wasn't Scotland Yard, despite the revolving sign, resembling a triangular toffee-apple, which proclaimed it as such. It was just another of London's vast new office blocks, so many chunks of masonry and sheets of glass slotted together like a child's toy.

He was a traditionalist and he regretted the move from the old Yard building on the Embankment. But then he'd never had to work in it and could afford to be sentimental, like those who mourn the demolition of a thatched cottage without light or water, never having had to live in one.

He entered, made himself known at one of the reception desks and walked over to the bank of lifts.

The impression of being in a vast office block was heightened as he glanced about him. The place teemed with young clerks of both sexes. So much so that the elderly constable on duty in the lobby gave the appearance of having strayed off his beat. Indeed, Adams wondered whether he hadn't been borrowed from Tussauds to add an authentic touch.

He shared the lift with a youth in shirt-sleeves who was clutching a bundle of files to his chest and a coloured girl with a tea trolley.

When he got out, he turned along a corridor which seemed to stretch as far as the eye could see. All sound was absorbed, save the hum of the air-conditioning, and the rows of identical doors had the appearance of being multiplied by the use of mirrors.

He stopped in front of one of them and knocked. It was the room of the secretary of the Commander, C.I.D., who ranked second to the A.C.C. in C Department.

'The Commander is expecting you. Go straight in,' said

the secretary, indicating the door which led into the adjoining room.

Adams walked across and knocked on it.

'Come in' a large voice boomed. Its owner was a large man with a shrewd mind and a wealth of experience, who had joined the Metropolitan Police as a constable thirty-five years ago and risen to his present rank by sheer hard work and ability. Adams had first met him when he had been a Detective Chief Inspector in the Flying Squad. 'Hello, Ted, stick your hat over on one of those pegs and come and sit down.' He pushed a stack of files to one side of his desk. 'I'm slowly getting buried under paper. All of us are. I sometimes wish the typewriter had never been invented, not to mention all these new-fangled copying machines. They churn out enough paper to fill an ocean.'

Adams nodded in sympathy. 'I'm sorry to have to bother you, sir.'

'Don't apologise. If it wasn't you, it'd be somebody else and, anyway, it's a relief to get my nose out of a file.' He lit a cigarette and pushed the packet across to Adams. 'So your chap got off!'

'Yes, sir.'

'Not altogether surprising. It wasn't a very strong case. You're always up against it when you can't prove a motive. And here you had the further difficulty that we couldn't establish any link between Laker and the dead man.'

'Undoubtedly, those were the two matters which undid us, sir.'

'Which brings us to the reason for your visit here!'

'Yes, sir.'

'You want to continue the investigation, eh?'

'Yes, sir.'

'Do you still think Laker did it?'

Adams realised that much was going to depend on his answer to this question. If he replied affirmatively, he would almost certainly be denied the opportunity he sought. It was only by expressing doubt that he was likely to get permission to go ahead. Further inquiries after an acquittal could lead those concerned into an extremely sensitive realm. The realm of public criticism in press and parliament with charges of vindictiveness and persecution, if it appeared that such inquiries were directed at proving a jury's verdict to have been wrong.

'As you yourself said, sir, it wasn't a very strong case and the jury's verdict may have been the right one, not only on the evidence, but in fact.'

'So you think someone, other than Laker, may have murdered old Dimitriu.'

'It's a possibility which needs further investigation, I think, sir.'

'Why are you so keen to reopen the case?' The Commander hunched himself forward and watched Adams keenly.

'Because it has so many unexplained ends, sir. Too many for comfort. I think justice requires that something further be done.'

'Justice for whom?' the Commander asked baldly.

'For the public, and also for Laker himself.'

'Supposing your further inquiries show conclusively that Laker did it?'

Adams shrugged. 'Well, even that, sir, will be something gained, although we shan't be able to do anything about it.'

'Personally, I've always thought that business partner of his knew more than he let on.'

'And he's not the only one! It was Mr Sherway who called in the case of the silent liars. They've *all* lied by keeping silent on one vital issue or another, including Laker.'

'You've no proof of that?'

'No, sir, but I'm darned certain I'm right. I must be right! If each of them had told me everything he knew, there wouldn't be all these unexplained ends.'

'Who do you include in your condemnation?'

'Laker himself, Reyman whom you've just mentioned, and old Mrs Dimitriu and her son.'

'They're the only ones we know about,' the Commander said, as though thinking aloud.

'Sir?'

'Well, it's possible, isn't it, that there are characters involved in this case whose faces haven't even appeared?'

'I suppose it's possible, sir,' Adams replied dubiously. 'But I'm not expecting my further inquiries to unearth new names, just clear some of the fog surrounding those we do know. That is, sir, if I'm allowed to make further inquiries!'

'You're going to have to make them bloody tactfully.'

'Yes, sir.'

'For God's sake don't let anyone find out what you're up to.'

'No, sir.'

'Because if anyone does find out, we're liable to be shot at from several directions at once.'

'I realise that, sir. Obviously, the Dimitrius and Reyman and even Laker will have to know . . . '

'Are you crazy, Ted?'

'What I had in mind, sir, was that I would make it appear to each that I was doing this in their particular interest.'

'Hmm! I should have thought that was stretching even your cunning a bit far. But the main thing is not to let the press get hold of a story.'

'I'm sure I can handle it discreetly, sir.'

'You better had!'

'I really do feel it's necessary to have a further investigation, sir . . . '

'O.K., Ted, I've said "yes". Don't try and overpersuade me.'

Adams grinned. 'Do you want me to report direct to you, sir?'

'I want to be kept fully in touch all along the line. And if you have any doubts about any particular gambit, have a word with me before you take any action.'

'I will, sir.'

'Heaven knows how you're going to set about it . . . or what you'll end up uncovering. Though I suspect precious little.'

Adams thought he was probably right, but at least it wouldn't be for want of effort.

Normally, he shrugged off his cases once they were over, whatever the outcome. It was the only way. But the murder of Gheorge Dimitriu defied such dismissal. It had set up a powerful irritant in his mind which only a discovery of the truth would dissolve.

II

Mrs Dimitriu jumped up from the sofa as soon as the telephone started to ring. It must be Peter. He'd promised that he would call if he was not back by seven o'clock and it was now a quarter past. She was impatient for news of what he'd been able to find out.

It was the day after Chris' acquittal, the same day on which Detective Chief Inspector Adams paid his visit to Scotland Yard.

'Yes?' she said in her throatily guttural English as she placed the phone firmly against her ear.

'Is that you, Gabriella?'

Mrs Dimitriu frowned as she recognised the voice of a distant cousin who was married to a psychiatrist and lived in Wimbledon with three abominable children.

'What is it, Margot?' she asked crossly. 'I am expecting Peter to ring me any minute so I cannot speak to you now.'

'Don't worry, dear, I won't keep you, but I had to call and say how awful Max and I feel about the result of the case. To think of that dreadful young man going free!'

'Yes, you are right.'

'But whose fault was it, dear? Couldn't the police have done more?'

'I can't talk about it now, Margot. Also you will realise how I feel! It is painful for me. I think only of Gheorge.'

'Of course you must. Max and I are naturally also desolate for you. If you would like to come over here one evening . . . Max is, as you know, so understanding. Perhaps he could help you, Gabriella. Help you overcome your grief.'

Mrs Dimitriu raised her eyes to the ceiling in exasperated supplication. If there was anyone more tiresome than Margot herself, it was her husband, Max. It didn't require anyone as shrewd as Mrs Dimitriu to recognise him for the unctuous phoney he was.

'I will phone you, Margot,' she said with growing impatience.

'Promise me, dear, that you really will do that. It's so long since we met . . . And all these terrible things happening to you. Do you think you will stay on in the house?'

Mrs Dimitriu pretended not to hear the last question. She knew there was only one way of dealing with her tiresome cousin on the telephone. She just hung up.

'Stupid, inquisitive woman,' she muttered as she walked back to the sofa and sat down.

She picked up the evening paper, but found she couldn't concentrate on it. Throwing it down on to the floor, she began to pluck fussily at small bits from it which were now adhering to her dress. She was still wearing black, though something rather more chic than the widow's weeds she had daily put on for court.

In fact, she seldom wore anything apart from black, though sometimes relieved by trimmings of white. As long as anyone had known her, she had dressed in these two colours. Moreover, her feeling for them amounted almost to a fetish.

The drawing-room in which she was now sitting, was, for example, furnished entirely in black and white. The walls were white, the thick pile carpet was black though there were two long-haired white rugs in strategic places where dirty shoes were unlikely to tread. The chairs and sofas were upholstered in black hide or white hessian. On the white mantelpiece stood a gold clock in the shape of Atlas supporting the world, its works encased in a perspex globe. It was the only thing in the room not actually either black or white.

She turned her head sharply as she heard a key in the front door. A minute later her son came into the room.

He came over to where she was sitting and stooped to kiss her on the forehead. Her eyes followed him as he went over to pour himself a drink. Then returning to her side of the room, he flopped down into an armchair, thrust out his long legs and, looking across at his mother, made a grimace intended to convey that it had been a day in which little had gone right.

'Sorry I didn't ring,' he said, in a flat weary tone.

She made no reply, but merely shrugged. She was waiting to hear more important things than conventional apologies.

Putting a hand up to brush back some hair which had fallen across one side of his forehead, he said, 'He's moved already.'

'Could you find out where to?' He shook his head.

'He didn't leave a forwarding address,' he said in a sarcastic tone, 'which is hardly surprising.'

'And the girl?'

'Gone with him presumably. The person I spoke to at the address said that Laker never appeared there at all and that the girl packed their belongings, paid a month's rent and departed, all in less than an hour. She must have gone almost straight from the court and done so. Anyway, they weren't there last night and their room's already been re-let.'

'Who did you speak to?'

'The woman who lets out the rooms.'

'Did you tell her who you were?'

'I said I was a journalist after an interview. I didn't tell her my name. She was a cantankerous old sow who'd already had her fill of gawping strangers coming to the house and ringing the bell just to have a look inside, so she wasn't particularly glad to see me.'

His mother continued staring at him intently after he'd finished speaking. For several seconds he stared back at her, then he looked away and once more ran a hand across his high, sloping forehead and through the long, lank fair hair which lay flat against his head.

'The police will know where he has gone to,' she said in a decisive tone.

'They may or they may not. But we can hardly ask them, anyway.'

'Why not?'

'What reason would we give?'

'He murdered your father,' she retorted vigorously. 'Is that not a reason?'

'Not one that is likely to commend itself to the police.'

As his mother sat glowering at the carpet, Peter Dimitriu reflected, as he had on so many occasions, that though she had lived in England for over twenty years, she was still wholly out of tune with the British outlook and processes of thought. In her native Rumania, an approach to the police in such circumstances might not have come amiss, but in this country it could only excite a considerable degree of suspicion.

'Nevertheless, we must find out where he is,' she said, as though passing the finicking details to a subordinate. 'If we are ever to find out the truth, we cannot afford to lose sight of that young man.' In a ringing tone she added, 'And the truth we *will* find out!'

'It may be necessary to employ a private detective.'

'Ach, one of those seedy men in a dirty mackintosh! No,

not one of them! You must be our private detective, Peter.'

'There are private detectives who are neither seedy nor wearers of mackintoshes, and it'll be much better to have someone who is unknown to Laker. He'd recognise me from court.'

'Then you must act without delay. It is already twenty-four hours since he disappeared.'

'I'll see to it first thing in the morning, Mother. There's nothing we can do before then. It shouldn't be too difficult to pick up his trail.'

'Through the girl?'

'Exactly.'

'She gave evidence that she worked in a literary agency.'

'I know she did.'

'You can find out which one?'

'It shouldn't prove too difficult.'

'Good.' She nodded in satisfaction.

'I went out to see Wynstan this afternoon,' he said, and watched his mother's expression.

She glanced at him sharply. When he didn't go on immediately, she said, 'Peter, please stop this silly game and tell me what you learnt. I do not like being dangled in this childish way.'

'I thought I'd better break the news to you gently, that's all.'

'Then you do not know me very well, even though I am your mother. What is this news?'

'He thinks Father's gross estate will be in the region of eighty thousand pounds and that duty will account for over thirty thousand of that.'

Mrs Dimitriu sat forward, her hands folded in her lap. By not so much as a twitch of a muscle, did she reveal her thoughts.

'But the really interesting part,' her son went on, with a small strained smile, 'is that over the past eighteen months it looks as though he realised assets to the tune of more than three hundred thousand pounds.' His smile seemed to become a nervous fixture. 'And so far Wynstan has been completely unable to find out what he did with the money. The assets were turned into ready cash and the ready cash has vanished. It's certainly not in any of Father's known bank accounts nor in either of the two safe deposits he kept.'

'Could Reyman know?' she asked slowly.

He shrugged. 'It's as difficult, in some ways, for us to approach Alex Reyman, as it is for us to solicit information from the police.'

'I have never trusted that man,' she remarked vehemently.

'There's no point in jumping to conclusions, Mother. I think we must accept that the money has gone for the present. What we have to find out is where. And when we have discovered that, we can decide on the next step. It means going through every scrap of paper Father left. There must be a clue somewhere.'

'What about his business papers in the office?'

'I imagine Reyman has examined those fairly closely, though he says he has handed all the more personal stuff over to Wynstan. At least, that's what Wynstan told me.'

There was a lengthy silence, during which mother and son each pursued their own thoughts. Then Mrs Dimitriu rose and stepped over to her son. Looking down at his stretched-out form, she said, 'It seems that the truth lies deeper than we knew, but we shall still find it ... *still.*'

III

Janey couldn't remember ever having been happier than during the thirty-six hours which followed Chris' acquittal. Her state of euphoria was complete.

She'd even accepted without question his insistence that they shouldn't return to their old room, not even for one night, and had cheerfully undertaken the task of buying off the disagreeable landlady and packing up their belongings while Chris waited for her not far away in one of the small, shabby hotels which abounded in the district.

That night their love-making had transported her into a realm of such exquisitely potent pleasure that the end of the world could have come without her noticing. Far less did she notice (as she had so often in the past) whether he had kept back that fraction of himself which he seemed incapable of giving and which, afterwards, she always found herself worrying about in a jealous fashion. Though never for long.

The second night seemed as perfect as the first and she

secretly prayed that life could go on like this for ever, knowing that it couldn't, and even being fatally aware that it would be *she* who would break the idyll.

She woke up about six o'clock that next morning. Chris slept peacefully beside her, his cheek against her bare shoulder. She shifted her position, gently so as not to disturb him and stared up at the ceiling whose cracks seemed accentuated in the early morning light which filtered through the skimpy chintz curtains.

Chris gave a little sigh and turned his head on the pillow, so that her shoulder felt suddenly deprived. She moved her leg softly against his.

It was thirty-eight and a half hours exactly since he had stepped from the dock a free man and she had run into his arms with a choked sob which she had been so determined to stifle. Thirty-eight and a half hours during which he had made no reference to his trial, other than to express relief that it was over and to regale her with anecdotes of life in prison.

As Janey thought back over the hours since his release, she realised that not only had he said nothing about the case, but he had also refrained from mentioning the future, other than to suggest that they should spend the next evening looking for a new place to live. She had agreed eagerly, still not being in the mood to question him about anything; content merely to accept his presence with untainted joy. She knew, however, that soon she would have to start asking questions, not to be nosey, but to gain some idea of the plans he had for them. She didn't want to push or hustle him, knowing how ready he always was to live each day as it came. And one part of her mind told her that this was reasonable after the ordeal he had been through, while another part warned her that it was a state which was likely to persist as long as she allowed it.

She glanced at the sleeping form beside her and wished with a sudden aching longing that she could know his mind as intimately as she knew his body.

In two hours time she would get up and go to work, leaving him still in bed, probably still asleep. He would pass the day in agreeable idleness while she worked, and, in between times, fretted about the uncertainty of the future. For it was at this moment she faced up to the reality that the worm of doubt, never dormant for long in her mind, had reawakened and would niggle until set at rest. When she got home this evening, they would have to discuss things. She would insist. She must have some idea of what he was proposing to do.

She sighed heavily. The future just didn't seem to exist for him, not even one hour ahead.

But surely he must have some notion. And yet he had told her nothing.

IV

Chris turned over on to his side and then opened his eyes. He had been expecting to nuzzle against warm flesh, but instead his nose met the cold edge of a pillow. The room was empty and it was obvious from the light streaming in round the ill-fitting curtain that the morning was well advanced. He squinted at his watch and saw that the time was just after half past nine.

Rolling on to his back, he doubled the pillow behind his head and gave himself over to contemplation.

He wondered how much longer Janey's restraint would last and hoped it might be yet a little while. On the other hand, he thought it likely that she would soon start dropping hints about the future, hints which would later turn into out and out questions. He was prepared to break things to her gently, even though he had no intention of being talked out of what he was proposing to do. He hoped she wouldn't try and remind him, even indirectly, of the obligation she had placed him under by her moral and practical support during the trial. He knew it was mean to feel as he did, but the fact remained that he invariably bucked like a rodeo pony when anyone tried to kindle his sense of obligation.

He reached across to the small bedside table and picked up his spectacles and put them on. Then he had a luxurious stretch and reflected that it needed a spell of prison routine to make one appreciate a lie-in in a comfortable bed. It was a pity Janey's own sense of duty had taken her off to work . . .

He fell to wondering how much he would mind if they

75

broke up and decided that it was sufficient not to court a breach. He knew that she was in love with him, whereas he was merely very fond of her. He'd never been in love with any girl. It just wasn't in his nature. On the other hand, he'd never met a girl whom he liked as much as he did Janey and certainly the sex side of their life was as satisfactory as it could be. Despite her tidy, well-ordered mind and her constant urge to plan the future, she embraced sex with uninhibited enjoyment. Moreover, however unwilling he was to admit it (even to himself), there was no doubt that she had had a softening influence on him. She had made him less selfish, in that he accorded her a degree of consideration he'd never shown any other girl.

All this passed through his mind as he lay and stared at the outlines of the now rather faded parrots which adorned the wallpaper in serried rows.

No, he quite definitely didn't want them to break-up. The short time since his release had been sufficient to convince him of this. Equally, however, his mind was made up as to the immediate future, and nothing Janey could do or say could alter that, even if it did lead to a breach. And knowing Janey, that might happen, though he would continue to hope not.

He decided he would give himself another ten minutes in bed, then get up and go out in search of breakfast. One duty he would attend to would be to phone his mother. He hadn't been in touch with his parents since the trial ended and realised that this would be adding to their bewilderment and sense of hurt. His mother's, at least. He suspected that his father might be quite relieved if his son were to pass completely out of their lives.

He glanced quickly to left and right as he stepped out on to the pavement some twenty minutes later, but observed nothing to alert his suspicions. The trouble was he didn't know what to expect other than that someone was certain to make determined efforts to track him down. Of that, he was quite sure. The further trouble was that, so long as Janey remained in her present job, it wasn't going to be very difficult for that someone. He had already warned her of the possibility and given her a few elementary tips on guarding against it, but he realised she would be unlikely to shake off any experienced operator in that field. Moreover, while she had listened intently to what he said and had promised to be careful, he also realised that once the questions started, this bit of cloak-and-daggery was in itself going to be the source of a fair number.

He turned into the doorway of a garishly lit establishment called The Golden Omelette and went and sat down at a table well away from the window. It wasn't very full and the rather shifty looking youth in chef's garb who presided over a row of chromium grilling devices grimaced on receipt of Chris' order. With reluctance, he put down *The Sporting Times* and threw Chris an insolent glance, at the same time idly beginning to pick his nose.

Chris watched him while he waited for his breakfast to come. He wouldn't mind betting ten bob that the youth had a record; moreover, one that was likely to lengthen with every few years he lived. It amused him to reflect that he'd probably be given far more enthusiastic service if he'd been recognised or had casually let drop 'that he'd just been acquitted of murder. However, he was thankful, in fact, that no photographs of him had appeared in the press, if only because they'd been unable to get hold of any. Moreover, on his discharge from custody, the police had helped to smuggle him and Janey away from the court, so that the waiting photographers had again been thwarted.

He finished his meal and got up to go. As he passed by where the chef was operating, he threw a sixpence on the counter.

'Buy yourself a present, you dirty little runt,' he remarked agreeably.

The youth scowled and seemed on the verge of answering back, but said nothing. Chris thought he might throw the coin after him, but this didn't happen either.

A hundred yards down the road there was a post office and Chris entered. Both the telephone booths were occupied and he went and stood beside the one in which an elderly man was making a call. He guessed he'd be less time than the mini-skirted girl in the other and proved to be right.

'Hello, Mum, it's me,' he said, as soon as he heard his mother's voice on the line.

'Oh, Chris!'

Fearing a burst of pent-up emotion, he decided the best thing was to go on talking as naturally as possible.

77

'Sorry I've not phoned before, Mum, but I knew you'd see from the papers that everything had turned out O.K. Remember, I told you it would.'

'Where are you speaking from, Chris?' she asked in a tremulous tone.

'From a call-box in Fulham.'

'But where are you living?'

'In a hotel at the moment, but not for long. I'll probably find a room within the next day or so.'

'And that girl . . . the one who gave evidence . . . is she with you?'

'Yes, Mum.'

'She sounded nice, Chris.'

'She is.'

'Why . . . why don't you bring her to see us?'

'I might do that, Mum,' he said in a tone which deceived neither of them.

'Chris, you're going to come and see us, aren't you?' she asked urgently.

'A little later on. I've got a few things to attend to first.'

'What sort of things do you mean?'

'I can't explain on the phone, Mum, but everything's going to be fine, so you're not to worry.'

'But how can I help worrying?'

'You just have to go on trying, don't you, Mum?' he said gently. 'But I promise I'll keep in touch by phone. And I definitely will come and see you when things are a bit straighter.'

There was a silence, but he could tell she was still on the line. He shifted awkwardly and waited for her to speak.

'Don't forget that I'm still your mother and you're my only son,' she said in a tone of weary sadness.

'I promise I'll not forget. And, Mum, I'm sorry for all the worry I've caused you. I really mean that.' She made no reply and he went on uncomfortably, 'How's Dad?'

'He's all right.'

'Fine. Well, look, Mum, I must go now. But I'll call you again in a week's time. Certainly before I . . . anyway, in about a week's time.'

'Before you what, Chris?' she asked anxiously.

'There go the pips, Mum. Look after yourself . . . ' He hurriedly put down the receiver and realised he was sticky with perspiration, and that this was not entirely due to the heat of the booth.

It had been worse than he'd expected. He had overlooked the fact that the trial culminating in his acquittal had been the explosion of an emotional depth-charge to his mother. The depth-charge itself had been present for years, but it had taken the trial to set it off.

He walked slowly down the street and was glad to come across a tiny park with two seats in it. The sort of place he would normally never have noticed and would have shunned if he had. On this occasion, he welcomed its ambience of decayed gentility and was prepared to share it with the scatty old man and equally scatty old woman who were presently in occupation.

He sat down at the opposite end of the seat occupied by the old man, who had the appearance of being wholly withdrawn inside a dissonant world of his own, which was the recipient of his aggressive mutterings and occasional fierce gesture.

Chris crossed one leg over the other and clasped a knee. How he detested emotional involvements! They left him depleted and, as a direct consequence, irritable. Perhaps it would have been better to have written to his mother. That would have saved them both. But he couldn't remember when he had last written a letter. Come to that, he doubted whether he'd written more than a dozen in the whole of his life, and over half of those had been to the same girl over a period of six weeks when he'd been a love-struck sixteen and she a pert fifteen-year-old who had gone to the same school.

'It's the eggs now! You want to watch it, young man. They're on the eggs.'

Chris turned his head to find that the old man at the other end of the seat was fiercely glaring at him.

'I expect you're right,' he said, with a placatory nod.

'Of course, I'm right. That's why they're after me. They know I'm on to their devilry.' Chris nodded again. 'When I let everyone know it was the bread, they changed their tactics. Now it's the eggs. Know what it'll be next?' Chris shook his head. 'Bangers! They'll put their stuff in the bangers. After that . . . ' He slumped wearily as if his one-man crusade required more strength than he was able to summon. Then with a sudden resurgence of vehemence, he added, 'But whatever it is, I'll be on to them. They won't get rid of me as easily as that.' He sidled along the seat towards Chris. 'I can be cunning, too,' he said with a leer.

'Good for you,' Chris remarked as he got up and made to leave.

'Going off for a quick swim, are you?' the old man called out after him.

'That's right.'

'Silly young fool, who's he think he's fooling,' Chris heard him mutter as he walked away.

Restored by a couple of pints of beer at a pub a short distance down the road, Chris decided that he would make one further port of call before returning to the hotel to await Janey's return from work.

He made his way to the nearest Underground station and bought a ticket to Victoria. As he pocketed the change, he made a face on realising that he was down to the last six shillings of the pound which Janey had given him. The grimace was not so much on account of his dwindling resources, as of the reminder that he had accepted the money since not to do so would have involved explaining a number of things he wasn't ready to explain. Though a moment of at least partial explanation was going to be forced on him shortly. On emerging from Victoria, he walked across to the B.E.A. office opposite and helped himself to a timetable from the rack.

Fortunately the place was full and nobody paid him any attention, which suited him since he didn't want anyone subsequently to recall his visit. Not that it was vitally important, but far better that they shouldn't.

It was on his way back on the Underground he discovered that the timetable didn't provide the information he wanted. However, a phone call to London Airport from Earls Court Station produced it and he wrote down details along the side of the newspaper he was carrying. He must remember not to let Janey see it or her curiosity would become unmanageable . . .

He was lying on the bed, hands clasped behind his head when she came in that evening. She ran across and kissed him, but resisted his attempt to pull her down on to the bed.

'No, not now,' she said.

'Not now what?' he asked, cocking one eyebrow at her.

'Not now what you were thinking. You had a look in your eye.'

'You shouldn't leave me for so long.'

'Somebody has to earn some money.'

Ah, so he had read the signs aright!

She stepped back from the bed and stared down at him with a worried expression. 'It's more wonderful than anything else, darling, that we're together again, but sooner or later we've got to discuss the future.'

'You mean, *my* future.'

'Yes, I suppose I do mean *your* future,' she replied quietly.

'It's not a question of supposing, you know you do.'

He couldn't help being provocative when she was in this mood.

A spot of colour appeared on one cheek. 'I don't think I'm being unreasonable,' she said. 'In fact, I think I've been pretty forbearing. After all, for two days we've not discussed the one thing which must be uppermost in both our minds.'

'Meaning, my trial?'

'Yes. What else?'

'What do you want to know about it?' he asked with a fixed half-smile on his face.

'I don't want to know anything in particular,' she replied indignantly. 'But you've never even referred to it. You've never so much as told me what really happened.'

'I was found to be innocent.'

'And are you?' she blurted out, now thoroughly riled by his attitude.

His smile widened. 'You should know, love. After all, you gave me an alibi.'

For a second she stared at him in disbelief then her eyes filled with tears and she threw herself down on the bed and buried her face in his chest.

'All I want,' she sobbed, 'is for you to tell me yourself that you didn't do it. Surely, our love requires that.'

He put a hand up and began to stroke her head. 'If that's all you want to hear, sweetheart, you shall hear it. I didn't do it.'

'Oh, Chris, you really mean that?'

'Of course.'

'I've been longing to hear you say it,' she said through further sobs. 'You've no idea how much I've longed to know it from your own lips.'

'Well, now you've heard it from my own lips,' he observed dryly. 'Anything else you want to know while we're on the subject?'

She lifted her head and looked at him with a frown.

'Now, what's wrong?' he inquired.

'You're not just saying it to please me? It is the truth, isn't it?'

'Honestly, love, what do I have to do? Light a candle, break a saucer and take an oath standing on my head? Yes, *it is the truth.*' For half a minute they stared in silence into each other's eyes. Her look probing, his parrying. 'Now, can we change the subject?' he asked hopefully and went on, 'Did you notice whether anyone tried to follow you when you left the office this evening?'

'There *was* a man standing in a doorway across the street whom I later noticed behind me near Piccadilly Underground Station. But I dodged about a good deal, which wasn't difficult in the rush-hour crowd and I'm certain there was no one when I got out at Parsons Green. Even so, I didn't come straight here.'

Chris nodded approvingly. 'Good. We must just hope that no one does follow you, though I'm fairly sure they'll try.'

Her expression clouded over. 'Why can't you tell me who *they* are?' she asked in a grating tone.

'Because I don't know, love.'

'You've told me absolutely nothing,' she went on, once more working herself up to an indignant pitch. 'I don't believe you really love me . . . you just use me. Nobody could have stuck by you as loyally as I have . . . '

With an inward groan, Chris jumped off the bed and gripped her by the shoulders so that their faces almost touched.

'Look, Janey, this isn't going to get us anywhere, least of all you. I've told you all I can. One day – probably quite soon – I'll tell you a lot more. In any event, I promise that you'll be the first to hear it. Meanwhile, you just have to trust me. If you can't trust me, that's too bad . . . I'm grateful to you for sticking by me, but – and I hoped you wouldn't force me to say this – I don't regard that as placing me under a ten-ton obligation.' He kissed the tip of her nose. 'It's one of the sinewy facts that in every relationship such as ours, in every marriage in fact, there's a giver and a taker. One gives more, the other takes more, and so long as the giver is content for it to be that way everything is fine. I don't mean that the taker doesn't also do a bit of giving, but if you analyse any male-female relationship, you'll find that it's basically as I say. In ours, you're certainly the giver. It's your nature. Just as it's mine to be a taker. At this moment, you're trying to upset the balance. I don't blame you for that, but, equally, I'm not going to be pushed into answering all your greedy little questions.' He kissed her again. 'But I'll tell you what I will do,' he went on cheerfully, 'I'll take you out to dinner and satisfy your other greed.'

She scanned his expression as if to detect a catch.

'And don't look at me like that,' he said with a grin, 'because what's more I'll pay.' He could see a string of further questions forming in her mind and added, 'I've got a job with an advance of pay.' He spun her round and pushed her towards the door. 'No questions now, but I'll tell you about it over a drink . . . It'll mean my going abroad for a short time.'

He felt her whole body stiffen, but by now he had a tight arm round her waist which gave her no opportunity of halting their progress down the staircase.

Well, at least he had broken the news to her. The next thing was to play it down, in particular the more dubious and dangerous aspects. Not that he intended to tell her more than the vaguest of details. The way to play it was to stress the shortness of time he expected to be away.

In fact, he had no notion how long the job was likely to take; though clearly longer now than it might have once.

v

Alex Reyman was puzzled. He couldn't think why the police should want to see him again and Detective Chief Inspector Adams had done nothing to satisfy his curiosity over the phone. It was obviously something to do with the case. But what?

He'd always understood that once a verdict was returned, that was that. It was finished as far as the police were concerned and they turned to the next case. And yet here they were, only two days after Laker's acquittal, wanting to come and see him.

Adams had been polite enough. Said he'd value a chat about one or two things and when could he call round, but Reyman had not been deceived. Any demurring on his part would certainly have come under immediate pressure, subtle or otherwise. The correctness of this inference, moreover, was underlined by the alacrity with which Detective Chief Inspector Adams had seized on his willingness to see him.

'I'll come over right away, Mr Reyman, if that's convenient.'

As well to find at once what it was all about, Reyman reflected, while he waited for the officer to arrive. Maybe he'd even glean something of interest to himself, though he would have to be careful not to show such curiosity as aroused the other's suspicion.

He gazed out of the window at the back elevation of a new hotel which cut off a good deal of light from his room. But, then, it was very much the junior partner's office.

Not that disparity in their working conditions had ever bothered him. Less still now when the whole business had virtually evaporated with Dimitriu's death. He'd salvaged his own small slice of the whole and then decide what to do. But meanwhile ... well, meanwhile, he'd keep things turning over until all outstanding matters had been cleared up. And that might take quite a time.

There was a buzz on the inter-com and his secretary told him that Detective Chief Inspector Adams and Detective Sergeant Paget had arrived.

'I thought you might have moved into Mr Dimitriu's room,' Adams said affably, as he came across to shake hands. 'You know Detective Sergeant Paget?'

Relman and Paget nodded at one another.

'How's business?' Adams inquired as he sat down. He gazed around him as if to note any changes since his last visit, which had been shortly after Dimitriu's death.

Reyman shrugged. 'Without Mr Dimitriu, there isn't a

great deal left. It was his creation and it more or less died with him.'

'Funny that he never took in any partners, apart from yourself. Thought he might have built it up into one of these property empires one's always reading about.'

'He could have done, but he just didn't have the desire. He liked to run it as a one-man show, and he was ready to devote his energies to that end.'

'We've certainly heard that he made a packet out of his various deals,' Adams commented wistfully. 'Pity police officers can't do the same.'

'Then they wouldn't be police officers.'

'That's true.' Then without change of tone, he asked, 'Any idea what's happened to the money?' Reyman shook his head slowly, and Adams went on, 'I imagine you know as well as anyone that a large proportion of his wealth seems to have disappeared?'

'I gathered something of the sort from the questions Laker's lawyer was asking.'

'That, if I may say so, Mr Reyman, is an extremely cautious answer. Surely you must have known something long before the trial.'

'*Know*. No, I didn't know. I had one or two suspicions that he might be funnelling off money, but it was none of my business and I didn't ask any questions.'

Adams concentrated his attention on lighting a pipe and said nothing for a few seconds. 'I confess, Mr Reyman, that I've never quite understood where you *do* fit in. You speak of Mr Dimitriu running a one-man show and yet you were his business partner. How did you come to join forces?'

Reyman was thoughtful for a time. 'We first met about twelve years ago. It was just after Dimitriu had pulled off a deal in the course of which he'd put a fair number of noses out of joint. They were the noses of people who weren't averse to strong-arm methods and, as a result, Dimitriu began to receive threats, veiled and not so veiled. As I say, we happened to meet about this time and he thought that, if we struck up an alliance, his disgruntled competitors might think twice before they started anything.'

'He took you into business as a bodyguard, in fact?'

'Bodyguard or insurance policy, call it which you like.'

'And it worked?'

'Oh yes, it worked very well. Mind you, don't get the wrong impression, I'm not just a bouncer, whatever I may look like. I'm pleased to think that I have a reasonable business head on my shoulders, as well. Anyway, Gheorge Dimitriu thought so.' His large craggy face broke into a grin. 'It proved to be an arrangement which suited us both very well.'

'How much business did you yourself actually handle?'

'Not enough! I think Dimitriu was frightened that I might become too powerful; might get too big a say in things. He liked just to feed me bits and push me forward when he was dealing with any of the wickeder boys.'

'Can I ask what the financial arrangement was between you?'

Reyman pondered for several seconds, while he stared hard at Adams.

'First, I think it's time I asked you a question, Chief Inspector,' he said at length, thrusting out his chin.

'Go ahead.'

'The real reason for your visit?'

'Oh, is that all!' Adams remarked with a laugh. 'There's nothing very secret about that. We're just trying to tie up some of the loose ends of the case. It had more than its proper share and, in one sense, the verdict created a few more.'

'You mean that you think Laker really was innocent?'

'It's not for me to express any views about that. Indeed, it'd be dangerous to do so. But most of the unexplained mysteries of the case centre on the character of the dead man and so we're trying to find out a bit more about him. You're an obvious person to talk to in that connection.'

Adams had tried to sound convincing and disarming at the same time. While he had no reason to think that Reyman knew anything more about Dimitriu's death than he'd already told the police, he was equally sure that he had kept back various details of his association with the dead man. Details which would help complete the jigsaw of Gheorge Dimitriu's life and death.

'I see,' Reyman said thoughtfully. 'You're just on a general fishing expedition, in fact?'

'That's it.'

'Hmm! Have you seen Mrs Dimitriu or her son yet?'

'No.'

'Or anyone else?'

'You're the first, if you must know,' Adams said a trifle irritably.

Reyman pursed his lips and studied the tip of the long silver paper-knife which he'd been playing with since the interview began.

'I don't see how details of my financial arrangements with Dimitriu are going to help you,' he said with a trace of defiance.

'They'll tell us something about the dead man. Something which may provide a clue to one of the unexplained features of his death.'

'They won't do that. You can take my word for it.'

'You'd prefer not to answer the question?'

'I'm not going to answer it because it's none of your bloody business. If I thought it'd assist you, I'd tell you, but it won't.'

'It might do.'

'It won't, so let's get on to your next question if you have any more.'

'Did Dimitriu often talk to you about his wife and son?'

'No.'

'So far as you know, was it a happy relationship?'

'I don't know about *happy*. I doubt whether it was in the temperament of either of them to be happy, but it was a settled one. I never heard of quarrels, if that's what you mean. But I'm not saying they never quarrelled, because I just don't know.'

'What do you know about Peter Dimitriu?'

'A good deal less than you, I imagine. I only met him socially from time to time. I never much cared for him. But then there are quite a lot of people I don't much care for,' he added with the note of truculence which had crept into his tone.

Adams peered into the bowl of his pipe, as if to find better answers to his questions than he was currently receiving.

'I'm sure you must have some theories about the case,' he said, leaning forward and speaking with a confidential air. 'I'd be interested to hear them. In particular, theories as to the motive.'

Reyman stared back at him speculatively for a full half minute.

'Yes, I have a theory all right,' he said at length, slowly. 'I think Dimitriu was secretly engaged in some deal none of us know anything about; and it's there you'll find the motive for his murder.'

'What sort of deal?'

'I've no idea. You asked me for my theory and that's it.'

'Do you think Laker was involved in this deal?'

'Obviously he could have been, couldn't he?'

'Hmm.' Adams frowned thoughtfully.

'Don't tell me, Chief Inspector, that much the same idea hasn't crossed your mind?'

'Oh, it certainly has, but the aspect which puzzles me is that we've not found so much as the faintest smell of a clue, I'd have expected to have come across some sort of lead, but no, not a thing. That's why we came unstuck over Laker. There was good, solid evidence of his presence in Dimitriu's car and yet we couldn't begin to prove any sort of association between him and the dead man. Also, Laker's hardly the type of person you'd expect to find caught up in secret deals with a wealthy businessman like Dimitriu.'

Reyman gave a faint shrug. 'I'd still keep my eyes fastened on him, if I were you.'

'Perhaps others have the same idea,' Adams observed.

'How do you mean?' Reyman asked sharply.

'I wouldn't have thought my remark required any explanation, Mr Reyman.' Adams got up. 'Let me know if you think of anything which might help,' he went on pleasantly. 'Any detail, however small, may be important.' He walked across to the door, then pausing, with his hand on the knob, turned back. 'Incidentally, it would be better if you didn't mention our visit to anyone.'

But Reyman's expression remained uncommunicative.

'Well, sir, what do you make of him?' Sergeant Paget asked when they were in the street.

'I don't know whether we learnt anything or not,' Adams replied slowly. 'Difficult to tell with a chap like that who's used to masking his thoughts. It was interesting to have his theory. He's obviously keen we should look beyond his own backyard for our motive. And beyond the family's too, for that matter.'

'From his reaction, he's certainly interested in Laker's next jump,' Sergeant Paget remarked.

Adams nodded. 'Aren't we all!'

Back in his office, Reyman was reviewing the game of poker (for so he regarded it) which he and Detective Chief Inspector Adams had played.

On the whole, he felt reasonably satisfied with the way he had played his hand. The only catch lay in how much more the police knew than they'd disclosed.

He was glad, however, that they still appeared to know nothing of the one thing which would have undoubtedly caused them to focus much stronger (and unwelcome) attention on him.

For that he had to thank fate. Fate which had removed Gheorge Dimitriu's faithful secretary with a virus pneumonia only two weeks before her employer's own death.

VI

Chris gazed about him uneasily. He felt jumpy and the impersonal hub-bub of the departure lounge at Heathrow Airport only served to feed his state of anxiety. Almost any of the several hundred people there might be tailing him.

For several days now he'd been certain that his movements were under discreet surveillance and though he had done everything he knew to shake off an unwanted shadow, including a move to a new address, he was far from confident that he'd been successful.

His journey to the airport this morning had been elaborately conceived and had required a couple of hours with all the precautions he had taken not to be followed.

And yet he still couldn't be certain. Worse, he was unsure to what extent his fears were neurotic or genuinely based.

'Excuse, please,' a voice beside him said, 'are you with the plane to Milano?'

Chris turned sharply to find a sinister-looking man in dark glasses and a camel-hair coat at his side.

'No,' he muttered, shaking his head.

'It is called, yes?'

'I don't know, I'm afraid.'

The man hurried away and Chris saw him go up to one of the girls on duty. Why hadn't he approached her in the first place? And why was he wearing a camel-hair coat on a warm summer's day? And who was that woman with a long face and a sallow complexion, also in dark glasses, who kept looking in his direction?

He wished now he hadn't given himself so much time. It would have been better to have cleared Customs and Immigration only just before the flight was called, though the final departure lounge had seemed to hold out the promise of Sanctuary that a church did to an escaping felon in the middle ages.

He would be glad when he was on the plane. At least there'd be fewer people to keep an eye on and it should be easier to pick out anyone showing an abnormal interest in him. But then he realised that once they were airborne, his shadow could also relax, knowing that Chris was, so to speak, in baulk until they arrived at the other end.

He got up, went across to the bar and ordered a brandy. Perhaps that would help to steady his nerves. The last few days had been bloody awful, not helped by Janey's alternating moods of silent reproach and passionate pleading to be told where he was going and what he was going to do when he got there. On the whole, the passionate pleading had been the easier to deal with, for, even though he had refused to satisfy her questions, he had managed to persuade her that such refusal was based on a desire to protect them both. Protect them from what she had wanted to know and he had spoken in a confiding tone of the necessity for absolute secrecy and of the pressures to which she might become exposed if it were believed she knew where he was, and of the dangers which would then encompass him.

At all events, whatever her feelings about him had been, her mood in bed last night had been one of passionate reconciliation and this morning it had been she who had radiated cheerful confidence when they parted.

He ordered another brandy and gulped it down, keeping his eyes fixed all the while on one of the television screens used for announcing flight departures. Surely it must come up any minute now. Nothing had been said about a delay and there was only twenty minutes to go.

Then suddenly there it was. A Swissair flight to Zurich . . .

The plane was less than three-quarters full and Chris had no one in the other two seats of his row. Across the aisle sat two nuns, whom he studied covertly before becoming finally satisfied that they were precisely what they appeared to be.

Neither the man in the camel-hair coat nor the sallow female was on board and a quick survey of his fellow-passengers as they'd walked to the plane had revealed no one of suspicious mien. There were a number of very obvious businessmen and several large families with small children in tow. By no stretch of imagination could the businessmen have been private eyes unless the breed was at complete variance with all Chris' preconceived ideas. Anyway, no private detective could look quite as sleek and cosmopolitan as these well-manicured and expensively dressed travellers.

Nevertheless, he was not proposing to lower his guard . . .

The flight to Zurich, however, proved to be as uneventful as a Sunday stroll, and Chris noted with considerable relief on arrival that it appeared to be the final destination of all his fellow-passengers.

He, alone, made his way to the transit lounge to await a connecting flight.

In a mood of euphoria he went and changed some money and then examined the offerings of the gift shop. He wondered if anyone ever did buy wrist-watches worth hundreds of pounds there. Perhaps home-bound millionaires who suddenly remembered they were short of a present for the second chauffeur or an indigent relation.

He felt tempted to put through a phone call to Janey, but decided this could prove incautious. Instead, he bought himself a brandy and, leaning against the bar, watched a group of passengers streaming out to a plane bound for New York. They were followed by another group bound for Tokyo.

What an extraordinarily impersonal business air travel was. One minute you were standing beside someone at a bar, the next you watched them walk out of your life towards the other side of the world.

Chris finished his drink and moved to a better position for observing departure notices. He didn't altogether trust his ear to catch the disembodied announcement which he knew would also be made. The woman making them appeared to have a bad cold and to be sitting in a cave when it came to the English translation.

Five minutes later, he was one of twelve passengers being ferried out to a waiting D.C.9. In another five minutes they were airborne.

In a few hours time he'd be in Bucharest.

VII

Mrs Dimitriu reminded Chief Inspector Adams of one of those matriarchal figures, beloved of a certain type of film, whose astringent comments on the surrounding scene only serve to conceal their deep-lying love of life's under-dogs. Save that, in the case of Mrs Dimitriu, he doubted whether there was much love of anyone.

She was seated bolt upright on the edge of a sofa in her drawing-room, eyeing Adams who was sunk none too comfortably in the middle of a huge arm-chair. She had rather obviously diverted him from the one in which he'd been about to sit (a white one) and motioned him to one of the black leather ones. Sergeant Paget had been waved to a hard-back one (also black) against the wall.

'You have come to tell me something?' she rasped.

'No, Mrs Dimitriu,' Adams said in what he hoped sounded a quietly apologetic tone, 'I'm afraid I have nothing new to tell you, but I'm hoping that perhaps you have something to tell me.'

'What is that?'

'I thought you might have remembered some detail or other . . .'

She shook her head impatiently.

'No, there is nothing. It is better now that you . . . you stop your inquiries. British justice has allowed the murderer of my husband to go free and that is the end of the matter. What more can you do *now*? All your questionings will only keep alive my sorrow.'

Adams tried to lean forward, but only succeeded in sinking deeper into his chair.

'Even though Laker *was* acquitted and even though he can never be retried, it isn't an end of the matter so far as we're concerned.

92

'If he was wrongly acquitted – and off the record, we think he was – we still have to try and tie up the loose ends.'

Her expression froze. 'My husband murdered! His killer free! And you speak to me of "loose ends". It is disgusting!'

'I'm sorry, Mrs Dimitriu, I didn't mean to belittle what has happened, least of all your husband's death, but I was referring to the various unexplained aspects of the case. For example, Mr Dimitriu's connection with the person who killed him. Who did he go out to meet that evening and for what purpose? As you know, the defence played on the fact that he was something of a man of mystery . . . .'

'He was no more of a man of mystery,' she broke in vehemently, 'than any other businessman. He was not British, you know, he was Rumanian by birth, just as I am . . .'

'Yes, I know, Mrs Dim . . .'

'So you cannot judge his outlook by your British standards,' she swept on. 'He came from Eastern Europe where business is conducted in a different way. There, it is not a big game of cricket. It is more like the chess. You do not tell everyone what you are about to do, not even your wife.'

Adams reflected on his own knowledge of British business methods and decided that even if deals might sometimes be consummated in the atmosphere of the cricket field, the negotiations were capable of being conducted with as much cold surgical precision as any Eastern European would be likely to match. However, he had no desire at this moment to get drawn into such a discussion.

'Since we're on the subject of your husband's business affairs, Mrs Dimitriu, do you have any idea how he got on with Mr Reyman?'

'Reyman was his partner, but, you understand, a very small partner. It was convenient to my husband to employ him.'

'Was it a smooth-working arrangement so far as you know?'

'Reyman did as my husband told him,' she replied imperiously.

It was apparent that she regarded Max Reyman as little more than a clerk and resented any suggestion of his equality with her husband.

'So far as you know, they didn't quarrel?' Adams pressed.

'My husband never spoke to me of quarrels,' she said, as though dismissing the notion that a king ever quarrelled with one of his humbler subjects.

'My impression is that Mr Reyman is a fairly strong character. He's definitely not what one might call a cypher.'

'My husband would not have employed him if he'd been *no* good.'

'Do you think he may know more than he has disclosed? More about your husband's business activities, that is?'

It was several seconds before she answered, then, rather to Adams' surprise, she said, 'It is possible.'

It was an admission he hadn't expected. 'Can you expand on that answer, Mrs Dimitriu?' he asked quickly.

She appeared to become once more lost in thought, and when she spoke it was as though she was thinking aloud. 'It is possible he has cheated my husband.'

'Do you have any evidence of that?'

'No, it is only what you would call a woman's intuition.'

'But even intuition is based on something, Mrs Dimitriu.'

'Intuition is a woman's seventh sense, Chief Inspector. I cannot tell you more. You come here and ask me to help you. So I give you this idea: it is possible that Reyman cheated my husband.'

'Are you saying that because you've since learnt that your husband's estate is less than you expected?'

'It is less, yes. I do not wish to say more.'

'And there is no indication where the assets have gone?'

'It is a matter for my solicitor now. He looks into the matter.' She made a movement indicating that she felt the interview had continued long enough.

With an effort, Detective Chief Inspector Adams prised himself out of the clutches of the chair.

'Will you let me know, Mrs Dimitriu, should your intuition become something stronger?'

'I will do anything to clear the mystery of my husband's death. I have sworn that.' Her voice carried a note of cold determination, which was not lost on the officers.

'I take it your son is not in?' Adams queried, though he reckoned they would have known if he had been in the house.

She shook her head. 'He is away. On business.'

'For long?'

'Some days perhaps. One does not know in his job. He is a freelance journalist and must travel often.'

'Where to this time?' Adams asked, with what he hoped sounded no more than casual interest.

'Germany and Switzerland.'

'What sort of events does he cover?'

'He writes many travel articles for magazines and goes to festivals and things like that.'

'Sounds an interesting life.'

'It is a hard one, being a freelance. It is not all a holiday as people think. And coming now when he has much work here at home with his father's affairs . . .' She made a small exasperated sound as the sentence trailed away.

As soon as she had seen the two officers off the premises, she returned to the drawing-room and, with a preoccupied air, plumped up cushions and emptied ashtrays.

She was thankful to have got rid of them before her son telephoned. It could have been extremely awkward if his call had come through with them still in the house.

VIII

Maricica stood on the terrace outside the airport lounge and gazed across the tarmac. It was dusk and the lights had been turned on. A faint, lime-scented breeze alleviated the stickiness. Maricica breathed in deeply. What a beautiful city Bucharest was, she reflected. What other capital was so deliciously perfumed by nature! It was her city and she loved it. On the other hand, there were other cities she wanted to visit, Paris, in particular. But it wasn't easy to obtain the necessary permits, not unless you were a privileged person in your own right or knew people who could help. And since Maricica was not a privileged person, she had been obliged to look around for someone who might be able to help her realise her ambition.

She folded her arms and moved over into the shadows at one side of the terrace where there were fewer people about. A summer's evening always drew crowds out to the airport to sit and drink and, for an hour or so, to enjoy vicariously the thrill of international travel. Not that it was a busy airport compared with the world's great, even though it did proudly boast the title 'International Airport'. But it was still exhilarating to watch the planes fly in from such romantic cities as Rome and Vienna – and, best of all, from Paris.

She moved yet deeper into the shadows and leant against a wall. She didn't mind if it did make marks on her white blouse, she needed to lean against something. She put her hand in the small pocket of her blue skirt and felt the two badges which she was later going to pin on.

It was a funny assignment and she wondered what lay behind the instructions she had been given. As far as she was concerned it involved nothing criminal, nothing worse, in fact, than a little harmless deceit. But the important thing was that, in return for her part, she had been given a promise of help in getting to Paris. Moreover, of travelling there legally and legitimately. That's where foreigners could assist, by underwriting your journey and making funds available at the other end.

The loudspeakers crackled into life to announce the departure of a local flight to Constanta. This was followed by an announcement that the flight from Zurich would be arriving in approximately ten minutes time.

Maricica decided it was time to go inside and titivate. She wanted to look her best. After all, she had a part to play and her appearance might be of some consequence.

She was short, built on the squat side, and had fair hair which she wore no longer than a boy's. Her complexion was sallow and her face on the puddingy side though redeemed by an extremely bright and lively expression. She mightn't be a classic beauty, but she certainly had no problem in attracting the opposite sex. There was something snug and cosy abour her which excited boys into thinking she'd be good fun in a hay-loft. About which some were right and some were wrong. It all depended on the view she took of those who entertained this kind of thought.

By the time she had finished renovating her appearance, the plane had landed and had taxied to a position in front of the airport building. She watched the steps being wheeled into position, then the door of the plane was opened and the first passengers emerged, blinking in the bright light which beat down on the apron.

Maricica recognised her man immediately from the

photograph she'd been shown. The horn-rimmed spectacles and the shape of the head made him unmistakable.

She thought he looked nervous and unsure of himself. Well, so much the better! It would make her job easier since he'd be that much more ready to accept her offer of assistance in finding accommodation.

As soon as Chris and his companions were lost to sight on passing into the building to clear Customs and Immigration, she went and positioned herself at the exit through which they would emerge. She was now wearing her two badges, one showing her to be an interpreter in English, the other to be an apparent member of a travel agency.

Chris came through the doorway and acted just as she had surmised he would. He put down the suitcase and proceeded to stare about him with a bewildered air. Unlike most of the passengers, he had no one to meet him and felt overwhelmed by a sudden onset of childlike alarm which can strike at those arriving in an utterly strange country, particularly one on the further side of the iron curtain.

This was Maricica's moment. She approached him with a warm smile and said in English, 'Can I help you?'

He gave her a startled glance, which quickly turned to one of almost canine gratitude.

'I've just arrived off the plane from Zurich.'

'You are English or American?'

'English.'

'And this is your first visit to Rumania?'

'Yes.'

'You have the arrangements already? Which hotel do you have?'

'I haven't made any reservations. I thought I'd look around and pick one when I arrived.'

Maricica pouted dubiously. 'It is not easy. There are many visitors in Bucharest now. And we do not have so many big hotels as London.'

'I didn't want a big hotel. I was hoping to find a small, quiet one.'

'I think I can help you, then.'

'I'd be most grateful.'

'How long you stay in Bucharest?'

'About a week.'

'As a tourist?'

'Oh yes, I'm here on holiday.'

'You will like it. It is very beautiful city and Rumanian peoples are warm peoples. You will find the gay life at night, too.' She glanced down at his suitcase. 'Come, we will find taxi and go to hotel.' She observed his hesitation and guessed the reason. 'You do not have to pay me any money,' she added with a laugh. 'We get commission from the hotel. It is part of the welcome to Rumania.'

'I wish more countries were the same,' he remarked, his final doubts dispelled by her open cheerfulness.

She led the way outside and in no time at all had hailed a taxi, a Fiat 1500 of battle-scarred appearance.

'I have told the driver to go to the Hotel Apollo,' she said as they started off. 'It is good, second-class hotel near to the Boulevard Magheru. Boulevard Magheru is one of the finest streets in Bucharest. You will like it very much.'

Chris was uncertain whether she was referring to the hotel, the street or the city itself, not that it seemed to matter.

'Is it far into the city?' he asked gazing out at the broad, well-lit road along which they were humming.

'Just a few kilometres.'

Indeed, they were soon in a built-up area with large villas on either side of a tree-lined boulevard, interspersed with an occasional modern building of Stalinist architecture.

'It reminds me of the outskirts of Paris,' Chris said, waving a vague hand at the scene outside.

'Ah, you know Paris?' Maricica asked eagerly.

'I've been there a few times.'

'It is very beautiful, yes?'

'I reckon everyone ought to see Paris once. It's unique.'

'And the Parisians?'

'A lot of grabbing monkeys.'

She looked puzzled. 'I do not understand "grabbing monkeys".'

'I mean, they are only interested in your money. They like you according to the size of your pocket.'

She frowned as though trying to reconcile this picture of the French capital with that of her dreams. Then she shrugged. After all, who were the English to cast such bricks?

'We are very proud of our Frenchness in Rumania,' she said. 'More children want to learn French in school than any other foreign language. Our culture has been much influenced by France. Rumanian is a Romance language. We are not Slavs,' she added, in case Chris was under any such misapprehension.

In fact, he was vaguely aware of these facts, though his knowledge was only of recent origin.

'Here you see our Arc de Triumph,' she went on as the taxi's tyres screeched their way round a mini Place de L'Etoile, and set course down another broad, tree-lined thoroughfare.

'Is it possible to get hold of a map of the city?' Chris inquired.

'Of course. You can buy one free at the Office of National Tourism.'

Chris laughed and she wanted to know the reason. 'You said "buy free". But if it's free, you don't have to buy it.'

She laughed, too. A pleasant, friendly laugh. 'You must excuse my English. It slips. I speak French better.'

'You speak very good English,' he said gallantly. 'After all, I don't know one single word of your language.'

After a short silence, she inquired, 'You will take tours, yes? You would like me to arrange?'

He shook his head. 'I prefer looking around on my own. I'm not one for organised tours.'

'What are you interested in in Bucharest? The Museums? We have many fine ones. The plays? Or the sport?'

'I just enjoy wandering around.'

'And at night? You do not wander around at night, too?' she asked with an amused smile.

'I just like to sit and have a drink and watch the world pass by.'

'All alone?'

'Not if I can find the right companion.'

Chris had been sizing up this particular situation at the back of his mind during the ride into the city and had reached the conclusion that, if opportunity presented itself, he wouldn't mind trying out Maricica's off-duty company.

'Are you ever free in the evenings?' he asked, turning his head to observe her reaction.

She smiled. 'Yes, I am free, sometimes.'

'Then perhaps we can meet and you can show me some of Bucharest's night-life?'

She nodded with apparent pleasure at the idea.

'Incidentally, my name is Chris. Chris Laker. What is yours?'

'Maricica Pungan.' She glanced quickly out of the window. 'Now we are in the Magheru Boulevard,' she said in her official information-giving voice. 'Soon we come to Hotel Apollo.'

A minute later, the taxi turned left and, after sixty or seventy yards, right into a narrow street of older houses of hodge-podge style.

The Hotel Apollo was a somewhat shabby, yellow-faced building with a dimly lit interior and a general appearance of worn utility. As Chris stared through the glass-panelled entrance door, an old man in a dark blue smock, who was sitting on a chair just inside, got up and came over to the taxi.

Maricica said something to him and he replied briefly, at the same time seizing Chris' suitcase.

'Yes, they have a nice room,' she said, turning to Chris. 'Here you will be comfortable and it is not costly. You will still have money to enjoy all the entertainment of our beautiful city.'

She had joined him on the pavement and now held out her hand.

'But I thought we were going to meet again,' he said, with the dismay of a small boy being deposited at school on the first day.

'If you really wish . . .'

'But, of course, I do. What about tomorrow evening?'

'O.K.,' she said, almost shyly. 'I will come here to hotel at seven o'clock.'

A moment later she had re-entered the taxi and it had driven off.

Chris turned and followed the old man into the hotel.

The lobby, if such it could be called, was empty and it became apparent that the old man was the only person on duty. He went round behind a desk at the far end and indicated that Chris should produce his passport, at the same time handing him a registration form to complete.

These formalities over he led the way over to an antiquated lift which threatened to plummet into the ground with the two of them inside. The old boy pressed a button and, after a considerable pause for thought, the lift began an uncertain ascent.

Room 19 turned out to be on the third floor. The old man unlocked the door and switched on the light which did little to enhance the immediate impression of austerity. There was a plain wooden bed, a chair, a lopsided cupboard with a cracked mirror on the upper panel of its door and a wash-basin from whose waste-pipe came sounds associated with acute indigestion. Moreover, the whole room was stiflingly hot.

The old man lumbered across to the window, tore back the flimsy curtain and, after a bit of a struggle, threw open the window.

For a few seconds he stood there inhaling extravagant lungfuls of breath, then he turned to Chris, who was stand-ing nonplussed in the middle of the room, and motioned him to join him.

'Fine luft,' he commented, taking another exaggerated breath. 'Comprennez?'

Chris smiled amiably and followed suit. Whatever the old boy had said, the air certainly did smell good. It was fresher than it had been and smelt strongly of lime blossom, and bore no relation to that within the room.

Satisfied that he had gained his point and could now retire, the old man bade Chris what he took to be 'good night' and left the room.

Chris turned back to the window and stood for several minutes staring out across the city. He could pick out the busier thoroughfares by the glow of light they cast sky-wards. Almost the only sound, however, came from a jukebox somewhere further down the street. It was playing a tune which had been on the British hit parade six months previously and hearing it helped to dispel the feeling of little-boy loneliness which had again begun to creep over him.

He turned listlessly back into the room and, lifting his suitcase on to the bed, started to unpack. As soon as he'd finished, he'd go to bed. There was nothing wrong with him which a good night's sleep couldn't put right.

Travelling always found him debilitated and melancholic on arrival, however much he might pretend otherwise. And on this occasion, there'd been not only a journey to a distant

101

country, but, also, all the nervous tension involved in the dubious enterprise upon which he was embarking.

At the bottom of his suitcase he found the street plan of Bucharest which he had brought with him. His inquiry about one to Maricica had been made from motives of simulation rather than of necessity.

As he opened it up, his eye fell automatically on that area which he now knew almost by heart.

'Parcul Herastrau', or 'Herastrau Park' as the plan put it in smaller letters underneath for the benefit of the insular English.

They had passed close to it on the drive in from the airport.

Tomorrow he would go there and look around.

He found himself trembling at the closeness of the prospect. Trembling with an excitement he'd not experienced for years. But excitement tinged with dark strands of nervous apprehension.

IX

After leaving Chris at the hotel, Maricica directed the driver to an address off the Calea Grivitei not far from the Nord Station.

She entered a new block of flats and went up to the sixth floor. The door on which she knocked was opened immediately and she went in.

'He arrived and is now at the Apollo,' she said to the man who'd let her in. He was short and squarely built, had well-oiled, but still unruly, black hair and a smudged upper lip which looked to be the only part of his face requiring to be shaved. The rest of it had a pale, waxy appearance.

'Any difficulties?'

'No.'

'Come into the living-room . . .'

She shot him a quick glance.

'He is here?'

'Yes.'

The man who had been standing over by the window turned as they entered and looked Maricica up and down in such an obviously appraising fashion that she became resentful.

'I should like a drink, Ion,' she said.

It was the other man who now spoke. He did so in Rumanian, though it was clear that this was not his mother tongue.

'Thank you for your help, Miss Pungan. I shall certainly be most happy to do all I can to assist you in getting to Paris. Everything legal, that is to say,' he added gravely.

'None of us wants to get involved in anything which is illegal,' Ion Cornescu said quickly.

'Exactly. And none of us will. Our concern is only with the illegal conduct of others; or, rather, of another.'

After Cornescu had fetched drinks, they all sat down.

'Did he tell you anything of his plans, Miss Pungan?' the stranger inquired.

'No. He just said that he was here as a tourist and wanted to wander around on his own.'

'Then we shall have to wander around behind him, Ion.'

Cornescu nodded. 'I'll go over to the hotel myself in the morning. If I'm there by eight o'clock it should be all right. He'll hardly set out before then.'

Maricica hesitated a moment, then said, 'He wants to take me out tomorrow evening.'

'Are you agreeable?'

'Yes.'

'Good. Excellent, in fact. You may be able to pick up quite a bit of interesting information. He's susceptible to the opposite sex and I'm sure you'll be able to win his confidence. Incidentally, I take it he didn't question your guise as an official of the tourist office?'

'I gave him no reason not to accept it,' she remarked.

'No, of course not. I'm sure you were excellent in the role.'

'Maricica trained for the stage for a short time,' Cornescu put in.

There was silence for a minute or so, which was broken when Maricica spoke.

'If I am to spend an evening with him, should I not know exactly what is going on?'

Cornescu looked across at the stranger with raised eyebrows.

'I assure you, Miss Pungan, that it is not really necessary. Suffice it to say that you will be doing a service to two countries, yours and mine, not to mention a service to each one of us individually, and that, of course, includes yourself. Laker is an unscrupulous and unprincipled young man. He has done great harm to my mother and myself and will do yet greater harm unless he is unmasked in time. I can only ask you to believe what I say. Ion, here, will vouch for me, if you have any doubts.'

Cornescu nodded vigorously.

A few minutes later, Maricica got up to leave. She shook hands with the stranger, whose name she'd still not been told, and was accompanied to the lift by Cornescu who kissed her on the cheek as he bade her good night.

When he regained the flat, he found his friend pacing up and down the living-room with a worried air.

'You're sure she's discreet, Ion?'

'Calm yourself, Peter. She is one of the most discreet girls in Bucharest.'

'I'm not sure that's much of a recommendation.'

'Don't worry. I have known Maricica Pungan since she was a schoolgirl. She will do anything that is necessary to gain her objective. In this instance, her objective is a trip to Paris and she will not do anything which might spoil her chance of achieving that.'

'Laker's a personable young man. Supposing he seduces her . . .'

Cornescu let out a laugh. 'Maricica's heart has never yet over-ruled her head, so have no fears. If she does get into his bed, it will be because her head tells her it will improve even further her chances of getting to Paris. This young man of yours will not suddenly knock her off her perch.'

'The odds are that some young man will do precisely that one day,' Peter Dimitriu observed dryly.

Ion Cornescu laughed again.

'Don't depress yourself, Peter. By this time tomorrow, we ought to have an idea what has brought your Mr Laker to Bucharest. Think of that!'

'Don't underestimate him. He's cunning. He'll do everything he can to cover his movements and to conceal the purpose of his visit.'

'But some time, Peter, he will be forced to disclose it,

Some time soon, too. And that is the moment we shall be waiting for ... '

X

When Chris awoke the next morning, one glance towards the window was sufficient to tell him that it was a perfect day. He could see a large rectangle of blue sky with one fat dollop of white cloud hung in a corner.

He felt refreshed, his spirits were high and the prospect of seeing Maricica at the end of a day in which he hoped to accomplish much sent them higher.

For several minutes, he lay back contemplating his course of action. The main thing was to appear normal and to excite no one's suspicions by behaving furtively. Although he had told Maricica that he preferred wandering around on his own, he must be careful not to give the impression that he was anything other than he pretended, namely a young man on holiday in a foreign city.

After he had washed and got dressed in a pair of fawn slacks and a dark red sports shirt, he went down to the lobby. The old man had been replaced by a youth with a spotty chin and a hairy upper lip which might one day turn into a moustache. There was also a prim-looking, middle aged man behind the desk who was sorting mail, as though it might have been bad fish.

Chris laid his key on the desk and went out, passing the youth who glanced up at him with a bleary look and a huge yawn.

'I know what your trouble is,' he thought to himself, as the youth slumped back against the wall overcome by the effort of moving his head.

Outside, the day was as delicious as it had appeared through his bedroom window. In a few minutes he had found his way to the Boulevard Magheru and to an open-air café where he decided to have breakfast.

It was pleasant sitting there, eating fresh rolls and honey and drinking strong black coffee, and he made no effort to hurry his meal. The pavements were crowded and the great broad road hummed with traffic and the air was again filled with the scent of lime blossom.

Eventually, he decided to stroll to the National Tourist Office which Maricica had pointed out to him and which was only a couple of hundred yards up the road. What more natural place for a tourist to visit on his first morning in town.

It was as he came within sight of the building that an idea occurred to him, for drawn up outside were a number of coaches waiting to set off on different tours of the city.

What better way could there be of approaching his objective! He could make his initial reconnaissance under cover of a group of rubber-necking tourists. Much more subtle than going out there under his own steam!

He entered the office and went up to one of the girls behind the desk.

'I'd like to book for the tour of the Village Museum,' he said, with an eagerness he failed to disguise. Happily, if she noticed it, which was doubtful, she'd most likely attribute it to a tourist's natural enthusiasm for the sights of her country.

She handed him a ticket.

'Bus number 3,' she said with the fixed smile of one giving away school prizes.

Chris found a seat at the back of the bus, lit a cigarette and waited for them to start on their way.

Ion Cornescu, who had had him under observation ever since he'd left the hotel, scratched his head in surprise.

Could it be they were mistaken about Laker? Here he was behaving like any relaxed tourist, rather than like someone who was believed to have come to Bucharest for a deeply sinister purpose.

For a minute or two, Cornescu hesitated. Should he also buy a ticket for the coach or should he take a taxi out to Herastrau Park and await events there? If he did that, however, it was just possible that he might miss Laker. Miss him, that is, if he was being really foxy and intended leaving the group at some intermediate point. But an inquiry soon reassured him about that. The coach went direct to the Village Museum and returned two hours later. No other visits were included in the price of the ticket.

Cornescu shrugged and went in search of a taxi. It was more important that Laker shouldn't notice him rather than he should have Laker under oppressive surveillance the whole time. Anyway, if the coach was going direct, there was little risk involved in letting him out of his sight for twenty minutes.

When eventually the coach did set off, it had about sixteen passengers. Their guide was a friendly faced young man who introduced himself as Dan and as a student of modern languages at Bucharest University.

'I tell you everything in English and French,' he announced, adding airily, 'And in any other language you want. I speak many.'

It seemed, however, from the reaction that English and French would suffice, even though Chris gathered that he was the only English passenger on board. There were some Swiss, a number of Scandinavians and a pair from India.

'Today,' Dan said, once the coach had achieved a less noisy gear, 'we visit beautiful Herastrau Park where is situated the fabulous Village Museum. Village Museum covers nine hectares of park and was built in 1936. It is one of the most interesting museums in all the world and has the aspect of a Rumanian village with about three hundred typicalish peasant homesteads brought from every region of our country. It will delight you very much, I know. Any questions?'

There were several, but Chris switched off his attention just as he so often had in the course of his trial. He gazed out on the pleasant leafy road along which they were bowling.

But three-quarters of his mind was elsewhere. Already in Herastrau Park impatiently trying to picture what awaited actual discovery.

He came out of his reverie only when Dan stood up and said they'd arrived. The coach rolled to a halt in front of a wide lich gate. They followed Dan through and clustered round him beside a diagram showing the lay-out of the park. Chris edged round to get a closer look at it while Dan was giving a short introductory talk.

'It is the most fantastic thing you have ever will seen,' he concluded, embracing them in the guileless warmth of his enthusiasm. 'Please follow me. But you can explorate by yourselves if you prefer.'

Chris decided to go along with the guide, since nothing could be less remarkable than that.

Indeed, it occasioned some surprise to Cornescu who was covertly watching them a short distance away. His relief at seeing Chris get out of the coach had turned to puzzlement on observing him idly strolling with the main party, stopping when Dan paused to point out a particularly interesting exhibit and moving on again when the rest moved. And so it seemed to be throughout the two hours spent at the Village Museum. Chris gave no indication of greater interest in one exhibit over any other. It appeared that whatever had brought him to Bucharest, the answer didn't lie in Herastrau Park.

In ones and twos they regained the coach, glad to sit down again and rest their dusty feet.

Chris tilted his head back, shot his legs out beneath the seat in front and gazed at the roof of the coach. No one would have guessed from observing him that he was in a state of almost unsuppressable excitement.

Everything had been as described to him. The Moldavian farmhouse with its frescoed walls, the cedar tree fifteen yards from the back door and the low mossy bank running from the tree to a small duck-pond and, behind the bank, the stretch of loose earth.

He had scarcely been able to refrain from revealing his excitement at the scene. Moreover, he couldn't believe that it would have appeared so exactly as described unless it had also remained untouched in what was to him its only important aspect.

The next step would be to return after dark and climb into the park at a suitable point. Once in, he didn't expect to run into trouble. It was very unlikely that there would be night patrols and the area he was interested in was well away from the entrance where one of the keepers might live.

Tonight he had his date with Maricica, but tomorrow night he'd come back and force an entry.

In the meantime, he could begin planning the next stage after that, which was going to be the most formidable of all.

XI

Detective Chief Inspector Adams felt doubly cross. Cross

because, despite all his arrangements, a day had gone by before he learnt of Chris' departure from the country and cross again when due to someone's stupidity or indifference he was informed that he'd flown either to Zurich or to Helsinki. And a fat lot of help that was!

The trouble was the usual one of people not under his immediate authority failing to be sufficiently impressed by the importance of his demands on them.

The fact that it was twenty-four hours before he heard that Chris had gone was entirely due to the message going astray – or rather to it having been consigned to the usual channels instead of being relayed to him direct as requested. Not that there was much difference between the two, he reflected as one savage thought chased another through his head.

Certainly there'd been apologies, together with pleas in mitigation. But it was of no interest to him to be told how many passengers passed daily through Heathrow, when his sole concern was with just one of them.

Accordingly, he was in an abrasive mood when he knocked on the door of Janey's room that evening.

When she opened it, he walked straight in, threw his hat down on a chair and turned around to face her squarely.

'I want to know where Chris has gone to.'

She hesitated a moment, as though deciding whether to react to his tone with her own display of defiance.

'I don't know,' she replied, shaking her head.

'I'm afraid I don't believe you.'

'It's true.'

'You mean that he's left the country without telling you where he was going.'

'Yes.'

'You're not going to tell me that you never asked him?'

She gave a small unhappy laugh. 'I pleaded, I threatened, I did just about everything save put a truth drug in his beer, but I couldn't budge him.' She stared straight back at Adams. 'So there, Chief Inspector!'

'All right, I believe you,' he said in a faintly grudging tone. 'But apart from trying to get the information out of him, didn't you have an opportunity of looking at his ticket or something of that sort? Surely you must have gone through his pockets, his wallet?'

'Well, since you expect me to have done so, presumably I can admit it,' she remarked wryly. 'But it didn't tell me anything. I never found his ticket. I don't know where he put it. Probably, he never brought it back here. As to his pockets, I didn't find a single clue. And it wasn't for want of searching.'

'Would his going to either Zurich or Helsinki make any sense to you?'

'None. I've never heard him mention either. Nor anywhere else for that matter.'

'What I'd like to know is where he got the money? Did you give it to him?'

'No.'

'And you've no idea where it came from?'

'No. He was as cagey about that as about everything else connected with his journey.' A puzzled expression slowly gathered on her face. 'But why are you asking me all these questions about Chris? He's done nothing wrong in going abroad. What's it got to do with the police where he goes?'

'Because we're still interested in Gheorge Dimirtiu's death and I'm sure your young man could help us if he were so minded.'

'But he's been found innocent. You can't try him again.'

'I'm not interested in trying him again, even if it were possible,' Adams said with a trace of impatience. 'But I'm darned sure he knows a good deal more than he's disclosed.' He paused. 'Aren't you, Janey?' When she didn't reply, he repeated, 'Well, aren't you?'

'Yes,' she said in a small voice and looked away.

'You don't have to be so reluctant about it. It's not a great betrayal, because it stands out a mile that this mysterious trip of his is something to do with the Dimitriu case. You realise that as well as I do. I just hope that he hasn't bitten off more than he can chew on his own.' He gave her a shrewd look and went on, 'I'm coming round to the view that he may be playing out of his own league and I just wonder if he'll be able to look after himself if and when trouble breaks. Because it's sure to be big trouble.'

Janey was silent for a time. Then she said, 'Do you really think he could be in danger?'

'I'm afraid I do.'

'But who from? I don't understand. Even if he has gone

abroad without telling anyone where, it doesn't follow he must be in danger.'

'What reason did he give for being so mysterious about his trip?'

She bit her lip. 'He said it would be safer that way.'

'Exactly. *Safer.* So he knew that he might be involved in danger.'

'I'm sure he wasn't going to do anything criminal.'

'It doesn't need to be criminal to be dangerous,' Adams remarked. There was silence while she digested this unpalatable observation. In a much gentler tone, he went on, 'But you may be able to help me, Janey.'

'In what way?'

'And if you help me, the odds are you'll be helping Chris too.'

'Yes, but how can I help you?'

'I want you to go through every possession he has and see if you can find a clue as to what has happened. And if you do come across anything, let me know. For example, look through every old scrap of paper he's left behind.' He glanced around the cramped room. 'It shouldn't be too difficult. After all, it won't be like searching Buckingham Palace.'

'I can't think I'll find anything helpful.'

'You never know. He's not a particularly tidy person, is he?'

'The reverse.'

'Then there's a chance you'll come across something. It's these obsessively tidy people who contrive to frustrate the processes of detection. I even remember a woman whose husband had been stabbed by a madman who'd burst into their house taking off his shirt and washing it before the police arrived. Not that it particularly mattered in that case, but if we'd come along a bit later still, the odds are we'd have found she'd have darned the hole as well.'

Janey laughed. 'Sounds a bit like my mother.'

A few minutes later, after receiving her assurance of help, Adams departed.

She was a nice kid, he reflected; even if, as he still suspected she *had* committed perjury at Laker's trial.

111

XII

It was a few minutes after seven o'clock when Maricica entered the desolate lobby of the Hotel Apollo. Chris was sitting on a bench against a wall of cracked brown paint looking bored. He jumped up with a smile, however, as soon as he saw her.

She was wearing an azure blue silk dress (at least, it looked like silk to Chris) with a short-sleeved jacket of the same colour and material. She had obviously spent a long time on her make-up and she didn't have a hair out of place.

She slipped her arm through his as they emerged on to the pavement.

'The hotel is O.K.?' she inquired.

'Yes, it's O.K.,' he said, without great enthusiasm.

'But I think you did not want a big expensive one?' she remarked in a slightly worried tone.

'You're right, I didn't. No, the Apollo's fine.'

'That is good, then. And now you must tell me, you have enjoy your first day in Bucharest?'

'Yes, very much. But it's not over yet.'

'Please?'

'The best part of my first day is still to come.'

She looked puzzled for a moment, then blushed. 'Oh, I see. Yes, we will have nice evening, I think.'

'Where are you taking me?'

'First to one of our famous park restaurants.'

'Splendid, how do we get there?'

'There is a bus . . . '

'Can't we go by taxi?'

'If you do not mind to pay.'

'It's a taxi, then. And what do we do when we get there? It's too early to eat.'

'We will drink and take a little walk beside the lake, perhaps. And after that we have dinner. You like dancing?'

'Not very much.'

'Rumanian boys all like dancing,' she said in a reproachful tone.

'I'm not very good at it, I'm afraid.'

'You need Rumanian girl to show you,' she remarked, giving his arm a small squeeze.

On the Boulevard Magheru, they found a taxi and she gave instructions to the driver. Ten minutes later they arrived at a wooden pavilion-like building set beside a lake. At one side of it was a terrace covered with tables laid for dinner, to which two waiters were putting finishing touches. Further tables could be seen inside the main building. The place seemed almost deserted.

Maricica led the way round the side of the building to a smaller terrace at the back which abutted the lake and on which about a dozen people were sitting having drinks.

They found an empty table and sat down.

'You must have a typical Rumanian drink,' she said gaily, as a white-jacketed waiter came up. 'It is called tuica. You know it, yes?'

'I'm afraid not.'

'But it is very famous. It is plum brandy.'

When the waiter brought the drinks, she lifted her slender glass and toasted him.

'Cheers,' Chris said and tossed his back in one gulp. 'Rather good,' he commented, running his tongue over his lips.

Later he insisted they had a further drink before going for a stroll beside the lake. Last light had almost faded by the time they set off and the water shone with satin blackness and the trees on the far side stood out in silhouette, so that they looked like a range of dark and sinister mountains. It was agreeably warm and the air hummed with the noise of busy insects.

They took a path between the trees. Chris slipped his arm round Maricica's waist and she responded by nestling closer into his side. As he bent his head to kiss her behind the ear, he felt that he had earned his evening of entertainment. A little farther on he stopped and drawing her off the path, kissed her on the mouth. Her lips were warm and soft and tasted of the plum brandy she'd just drunk. She neither resisted him, nor did she respond with discernible eagerness.

'Shall I tell you something,' he said, as they strolled on again. 'You're the first Rumanian girl I've ever kissed.'

'You make me sound like a new stamp in a stamp collection.' she remarked.

Chris couldn't tell from her tone whether she was amused or slightly annoyed by his comment. However, it didn't sound like an extreme of either, so perhaps it didn't matter which it was.

A large clock set into an eave of the restaurant showed nine o'clock when they returned. Most of the tables on the terrace were already occupied, but they found one over against a high trellis fence which divided the terrace from the car park.

Chris was content to leave the ordering to Maricica. Not that he was given much choice since she had seized the menu and gone into conference with the waiter.

'First we have mamaliguta,' she told him as part of the running commentary which accompanied the ordering. 'Then Sarmale which are meat balls in cabbage leaves and very delicious.'

'What was the first thing you mentioned?'

'Mamaliguta? It is boiled maize meal with cream and curd cheese. Or perhaps you prefer with poached eggs?'

'I think definitely not with poached eggs,' he said firmly.

'You will like,' she replied in confident tone.

The waiter returned with two glasses and a bottle of white wine, which he set down on the table after filling their glasses.

'To a happy time,' she said, lifting hers and smiling at him over the top of it.

'To Maricica,' he replied, matching the gesture.

She continued to smile at him.

'You are nice. Are all English boys like you?'

'Are all Rumanian girls like you?'

She laughed. 'No, it is true, all peoples are different. You are Chris and I am Maricica.'

'Where do you live?' he asked after a pause, during which they sipped their wine and glanced around at the other diners.

'I live with my mother and father in a new part of the city called Tonola. It is very nice.'

'Is there anything about Bucharest which is not very nice?' he asked, with a laugh.

She frowned. 'I do not understand.'

'You're always saying "it is very nice" about everything.'

'But it is very nice. It is my city. I am very proud of

Bucharest. Are you not proud of London?'

'I like London all right. I'm not proud of it. Come to that, I never think of it in terms of pride. It's just there all around me all the time.'

'You should be proud of your country,' she remarked.

'You be proud of yours and I'll just go on taking mine for granted,' he replied in a tone which made her look at him curiously.

'What is your work?' she asked.

Luckily Chris was prepared for this question, since he had considered it was bound to come sooner or later in the course of the evening.

'I work in a market research firm, if you know what that is.'

She shook her head as he'd assumed she would. One reason why he'd selected this occupation out of all the possibles.

'We find out why people prefer one product more than another.'

'Why?'

'So that the manufacturer can either change the product or its sales methods to meet competition.'

She made a face. 'Is it very necessary?'

'In a capitalist country, yes. For example, supposing the people who make meat balls decided they'd be even nicer wrapped in vine leaves than cabbage leaves, he'd want to find out. So he'd make sample tests. He'd persuade, say, the manager of this restaurant to serve them the new way and then he'd note the customers' reaction. Follow?'

'But it is crazy what you say. We already have meat balls wrapped in vine leaves. And anyway, each restaurant makes meat balls in its own way. There is no manufacturer of meat balls. They are made in kitchens, not in factories.'

'Perhaps it's not a very good example,' he conceded, 'but it gives you the general idea of market research.'

'It sounds dull.'

'On the contrary,' he said stoutly, defending a profession which he'd never had the slightest inclination to join, 'it's fascinating work.' She grimaced and he went on, 'Every business indulges in a certain amount of market research. It has to. I bet they do even in Rumania. For example doesn't your travel agency need to know why people prefer one holiday place rather than another?'

She had the grace to look abashed, but happily for her, their food arrived and she was saved any further embarrassment by being able to launch into a dissertation on the culinary aspects of what had been put in front of them.

A little later, she watched Chris refill her glass with wine and fell to wondering about him. According to Cornescu and the Englishman, whose name she didn't know, he was an evil young man who had come to Rumania for some unspecified wicked purpose. Looking at him now, she found this difficult to believe, though she knew well enough how deceptive appearances could be. But he had an agreeable face and a friendly manner and there'd been something gentle about him, too, as revealed on their recent walk. She had little doubt that he would try and get her to go to bed with him that night and she was, as yet, undecided what her reaction would be. Something warned her to be on guard against such a fast worker. In fact, she would have been considerably shocked by his advances, had it not been for her friend Florica who had spent six months in London as an *au pair* girl and who'd brought back tales of instant seduction at parties – often, almost before the party was under way.

Cornescu and the Englishman wanted her to try and worm out of Chris the reason for his visit to Bucharest. They had even hinted that, if necessary, she ought to allow herself to be made love to; certainly that she should try and loosen his tongue with drink.

'How many more main courses to come?' he asked with a glazed expression as the waiter brought them plates of skewered meat and a salad of mysterious green cubes.

'You like, yes?' Maricica asked, shaking off her reverie.

'I'm not used to so much food.' He had hardly liked to tell her that the first course had reminded him of Brixton Prison porridge on one of its better days and that the greasy content of the succeeding dishes had caused his stomach to reel.

He noticed that Maricica herself tucked into everything with zest, which undoubtedly accounted for the pneumatic feel of her waist. That was fine by him since he preferred his girls to be on the plump side. He couldn't bear those angular, bony ones. It was too much like taking one of those tubular chairs into bed with you.

When, at last, their meal was finished and the wine bottle was empty, he suggested that they should have some more tuica. Maricica nodded her agreement.

'Then you like to go to the night-club?' she asked.

'Let's think about it,' he said, smothering a yawn.

'You are already tired?'

'I always get sleepy at this hour, then I come to life again.'

'You are on holiday, so you can stay in bed tomorrow morning.'

'True.'

'Do you usually go on holiday alone?' she said suddenly.

'Quite often.'

'You are not lonely?'

'Not when I meet a girl like you.'

'But you might not meet a girl like me.'

'Then I may become lonely.'

'You are making fun at me.'

'Let's get the bill and go for a little walk and I'll show you that I'm not making fun of you.'

'Let us go to night-club. I know one near university. You will like. Music and dancing and fine entertainment.'

Chris shrugged. 'O.K., let's do that.' If he was going to be up the whole of the next night, he'd need to spend a part of tomorrow in bed.

A taxi took them back into the city and deposited them outside a doorway with a flashing neon sign. 'Capri' it read. A short flight of stairs brought them down into a crowded, half-lit room, whose walls were decorated with huge chocolate-box pictures of the Bay of Naples.

The atmosphere was compounded of deafening sound, heat sufficient to melt the dark glasses almost everyone seemed to be wearing and an amalgam of strong, sticky smells which it was probably wiser not to try and analyse.

Maricica manouevred herself on to the end of a padded bench and then executed a sideways wriggle to make room for Chris. Those already occupying the bench accepted the invasion cheerfully. Maricica shouted an order at a passing waiter and the next time he came their way he put down two glasses and a small flask of tuica. Chris would have preferred a cold beer, but it was simpler to accept what they'd been given than embark upon a rigmarole of explanation.

Maricica's face was glowing with pleasure as much as with warmth, as she raised her glass to Chris in a silent toast.

Shortly afterwards the floor was cleared of dancers and a spotlight was turned on to a curtained doorway. Through it came a short, pudgy man of uncertain age. He had thinning sandy hair, eyes like excited fireflies and a mouth which appeared to stretch from ear to ear.

He had hardly opened his mouth before his appreciative audience were seized with a merriment which continued unabated and seemed to Chris to bear small relation to the moments when he was actually saying anything.

'Very funny man,' Maricica gasped into his ear.

'So I gather,' he replied sourly. 'What's he saying?'

'It is pity you can't understand Rumanian.'

'O.K., but what's he saying?'

'He's telling story of peasant woman. She had old husband. And one day when her husband is at the market, a young man from the Ministry of Food comes to farm. But the woman thinks he is the son of her husband's cousin . . .' Maricica's voice trailed away as she turned her full attention once more to the speaker. 'I explain afterwards,' she hissed.

Chris, however, had already decided that he wouldn't press for further explanation since whatever humour there was in the story was clearly going to get lost in the translation.

Five minutes later the funny man departed to thunderous applause, his story of the peasant woman, her old husband and the young man from the Ministry, who wasn't the husband's cousin's son, presumably concluded.

He was followed by two buxom girls billed as Pam and Pru, who sang, in rapid succession, songs in English, French and Rumanian. They did so with fixed smiles and clichéd gestures, and wholly without distinction. Though their reception was less tumultuous than the comic's, it far exceeded their worth in Chris' estimation. He reckoned they'd have been lucky to have got jobs as barmaids back in England.

These two acts concluded, dancing resumed.

'You like to dance?' Maricica asked turning to him with an eager expression.

'Sure,' he said without enthusiasm.

Maricica pressed herself against his body as they staked out their claim to a few square inches of space. The top of her head came up to his chin, which made speech impossible, so he contented himself with letting his hands get on with a bit of seductive work.

When the music eventually stopped and they returned to their table, it was to discover that another couple were occupying their seats.

'Don't let's worry. Let's get out,' Chris said.

'But there is some more cabaret,' Marcica protested.

'I'll give you a much better turn,' Chris remarked, pulling her towards the exit.

'What is that? I don't understand.'

'I'll explain outside.'

When they reached the pavement, he stood and took several deep lungfuls of the freshly scented night air.

'That's better.'

'You not like our night-club?'

'Too hot.'

'So now it is time to go home.'

'Who says?'

'Please?'

'Why don't you come back to the hotel? I have a bottle of Scotch in my room.'

'It is not good.'

'What's not good?'

'I come to your bedroom.'

'Why not?'

'Peoples think things.'

'Peoples can think what they like, why should we worry?'

'I not know you very long.'

'Long enough.'

She giggled. 'I like you.'

'Fine, then come back to the hotel with me, because I like you, too.'

'But then you would think I'm not nice girl.'

'I wouldn't think anything of the sort. In fact, it would confirm that you're even nicer than I think.'

'Perhaps tomorrow night.'

'No, tonight.'

'Why not tomorrow night?'

'Because I can't tomorrow night.'

She pouted. 'You have another girl in Bucharest?'

'No, it's just that I have another engagement tomorrow night.'

'But you tell me you do not know anyone . . . '

Chris was beginning to feel irked by this cross-examination. He wished he hadn't laid himself open to it. He was also nettled by her show of reluctance to go back with him. However, if she wouldn't, she wouldn't. It would at least mean that he'd have a rather longer night's sleep.

'It's someone I met on the plane,' he lied. 'He phoned me and we're having dinner tomorrow evening.'

Even as the words left his mouth, he cursed himself. But Maricica did not notice his slip, and didn't ask him how the person had managed to find out which hotel he was staying at.

They had begun walking along the almost deserted street, when she hailed a passing cab.

'I see you again?' she inquired with her head on one side.

'Where can I get in touch with you?'

'I will get in touch with you. At hotel. But not tomorrow night when you are out with friend,' she said pointedly. She held out her hand. Chris took it and pulled her to him and kissed her firmly on the lips.

'Good night, Maricica. And thank you. I've enjoyed our evening.'

'I've enjoyed also.' She gave him a little wave as the cab drove off.

He passed his tongue across his lips on which he could still taste the tuica she'd imparted there. Whenever he wanted to recall Maricica to mind, all he'd have to do would be to imbibe again Rumania's distinctive national drink. But now to discover where he was and find his way back to the hotel.

A police car drove slowly by and the occupants stared at him with curiosity. But it didn't stop and, with its passing, Chris had one of those sudden unaccountable feelings that everything was going to work out in his favour.

It was with a confident tread that he set off down the road in search of someone to ask the way.

XIII

Alex Reyman arrived in Bucharest a few hours after Chris had gone to bed. Like most people he hated night flights but he had had to reach a decision quickly and, having reached it, he'd caught the first available plane in the right direction.

Now at half past six in the morning he was sitting on the deserted terrace of the Lido Hotel slowly stirring the cup of black coffee he'd managed to persuade the night porter to bring him and into which he had put five lumps of sugar.

As he stirred he gazed balefully at the swimming pool with its much advertised artificial waves, save that it was now empty of water and resembled nothing more than a large blue hole in the ground. Two buckets and a number of wide brooms lay on the floor of the pool. Together with a pair of flung-down waders, they gave the impression of some piece of still-life composition.

Reyman was no stranger to Bucharest and he had stayed at the Lido on each of his two previous visits. On those occasions he had come on the old boy's business and stayed four or five days each time. He had met Ion Cornescu and visited him at his flat.

A mean-faced cat stalked past the table at which he was sitting, pausing only long enough to discover that he had nothing to offer it, either by way of food or affection. He gave it a red-rimmed glare.

Despite his travel-tiredness he felt exhilarated and full of expectation. Anyway, his tiredness was something he could cope with. His naturally tough constitution fortified by benzedrine would see him through for as long as necessary. Moreover, he reckoned that events would move rapidly.

It had been less than twenty-four hours ago that he had begun to piece together the bits of information which had resulted in his journey.

First, he had discovered from Janey, whom he had telephoned on a false pretext, that Laker had gone abroad. Then he had learnt from old Mrs Dimitriu that Peter was out of the country. In Germany, she had said. Luckily, he knew the small travel agency which Peter Dimitriu always used and it had not been difficult to find out that, in fact, Bucharest was his destination.

And if Dimitriu had chased off to Rumania, it followed that Laker was there, too. It not only followed, it made sense as well, for Reyman thought he had a better idea than anyone of the purpose of Laker's visit.

There'd been a time, he was sure, when Gheorge Dimitriu had been about to disclose to him what, he was certain, the old boy had subsequently revealed to Laker.

And if he was right about this, he was damned if he was going to let that cool young man get away with the whole boiling. He'd got away with too much when he was acquitted of murder. He now saw Laker as a ferret about to descend on his prey, unaware of the circling falcon overhead who would deprive him of it at the vital moment.

The only thing Laker could know which Reyman didn't was the precise location of the prey and its exact content. Otherwise, he was sure he had worked everything out correctly. He was equally sure that the Dimitrius, mother and son, were almost entirely in the dark. They'd known for a time that something was up, but it was clear they'd not been in possession of the facts from which he had been able to make *his* deductions.

A wily, secretive old boy, Gheorge! It was typical of him that he had finally turned and enlisted the help of a stranger, even though it had been his undoing – his death, no less.

Well, Christopher Joyce Laker had better mind his step, since his run of luck was about to reach an end!

Reyman looked at his watch. It was ten minutes to seven and he glanced up at the façade of the hotel. There was someone at the second-storey window staring down at him. He stared back and the person moved away. It had been a man with red hair and a bared torso, which he had been vigorously scratching as he stood at the window.

He spooned up the thick, sweet dregs in his coffee cup and swallowed them. Then he rose and went inside. He'd go up to his room and have a wash and shave. After which it would be time to go out. He couldn't risk missing Cornescu, when he left the flat. And Cornescu would lead him to Laker. Of that he was certain.

Well, at least he had the advantage of neither side being

aware of his arrival. An advantage which he intended to keep.

He permitted himself a small grim smile as he went up in the lift. He wondered whether it was likely to come to rough stuff. The prospect certainly didn't bother him. He was prepared for every eventuality. So far as he was concerned, the end was going to justify the means.

In the conclusion, it would be every man for himself and Alex Reyman felt no qualms about his own position. Laker and Dimitriu were both amateurs by comparison with himself when it came to swift, ruthless exploitation of a situation.

A sudden frown formed on his brow as he turned the key in his door. Supposing he was already too late . . .

No it couldn't be! Events might already be on the move, but it was impossible that they were concluded. He'd lost only twenty-four hours, or a little over, and Laker couldn't have worked that quick.

As he shaved, he hummed in a dirge-like way.

XIV

At nine o'clock that morning, Maricica phoned Ion Cornescu.

'Where are you speaking from?' he asked immediately.

'Home.'

'You didn't spend the night with him, then?'

'No.'

'Well?'

'He's got another engagement this evening.'

'What?'

'He said he's dining with someone he met on the plane.'

'Did you see him talking with anyone when he left the plane?'

'No.'

'You didn't notice him in conversation with any of his fellow-passengers before you approached him at the airport?'

'No.'

'Then it seems that he must be lying.'

'Possibly.'

'More than possibly, I'd say. Have you made plans to see him again?'

'Nothing definite.'

'You don't sound very keen on him.'

'He means nothing to me.'

'I'm glad to hear it, if you mean what I hope you do. After all, it's not *he* who is going to underwrite your visit to Paris.'

'When can I go, Ion?' she asked anxiously.

'As soon as this whole thing is settled.'

'But when will that be?'

'In a week or two.'

She sighed. 'I hope so.'

'Don't doubt it. Dimitriu will keep his promise, provided you do everything required of you.'

'What do you want me to do next?' she asked in a subdued voice.

'I'll let you know. It depends on what happens today; in particular, this evening. You obviously can't see him in the daytime or he'll wonder why you're not at work at your travel agency.'

'I know.'

'We certainly don't want him to find out, do we, that you're an out-of-work actress?' She made no reply and he continued, 'By the way, I ought to have asked you before, did you enjoy your evening with him?'

'I thought you'd gathered.'

'Did you or didn't you?'

'It was not a wholly disagreeable job of work.'

'You sound like a lawyer, my dear.'

'I was only trying to answer your question.'

'A not wholly disagreeable job of work,' he repeated in an amused tone. 'Anyway, I'm sure you'll find Frenchmen much more romantic than English when you get to Paris. I thought he looked rather a dull young man for someone who . . . ' He broke off abruptly.

'Who what?'

He laughed. 'Who can rouse such resentment and ill-feeling in Peter Dimitriu.'

'What's he really supposed to have done, Ion?'

'Whatever it is, it's not a story for the telephone. And

now I must go. I'll get in touch with you tomorrow morning at about this time.'

'All right.'

After he had rung off, Maricica perched herself on the edge of a chair and stared mindlessly across the small cluttered room. So cluttered that moving around in it became a complicated exercise of ingenuity.

She wondered what Chris had really done, and what had brought him to Bucharest. She rather hoped she wouldn't be required to see him again, as she felt she might grow to like him more than would be prudent.

Once or twice last night she had had to remind herself that this was a job of work with a trip to Paris as the reward. Even so, she had found that her dream of the French capital had suddenly become less obsessive.

It had been in the middle of dinner when they had raised their glasses and drunk one of their innumerable toasts to each other that she had mentally pinched herself.

'Remember, Maricica,' she had told herself, 'you want to go to Paris more than anything else in this world. You've longed for the day since you were eight years old. It's now about to be realised. You know nothing about this young man. O.K., he's nice and he's fun to be out with. But surely you're not going to jeopardise your chances of getting to Paris on the strength of one flirtatious evening with an Englishman?'

At that moment, the answer had flashed up like a danger sign. 'Certainly not.'

XV

Chris was in no hurry to get up. Indeed, he didn't even bother to look at his watch to see what time it was. His bedroom was flooded with light and, from all the street sounds which reached his ears, he guessed the morning was well advanced.

On balance, he decided it was probably a good thing that Maricica had declined to return with him the previous night. It might have led to complications, which would be the greater for his being in a strange city. You just never knew with some girls. They were one thing out of bed and something quite different under the blankets. Maricica might have been one such; and this was no time for emotional entanglements.

He thought of Janey and wondered if she was thinking of him at this moment. As on previous occasions, she would by now have accepted the situation, if only because she had little choice in the matter. On the other hand, this wouldn't stop her, when she felt like it, working herself up into a paddy over his behaviour. He knew how much she wanted them to get married, though she was careful not to push this too far. She realised, perhaps better than he, that any sort of ultimatum might have the effect of driving him out. The fact was that he just couldn't envisage marriage. It was far too final for someone who liked to keep all his options open – and whose thought for the morrow was no more real than a polar bear's for a life on the equator.

He hadn't really thought about it before, but he suddenly realised that if everything now worked out to plan, his relationship with Janey would almost certainly be the subject of chance. There'd be no question of spinning out life in an Earls Court bed-sitter, for a start.

However, sufficient unto the day, even though it might be at hand! But even to think like that was being almost recklessly optimistic. By far the toughest part lay ahead. Success tonight would be no more than a first step and, as yet, he hadn't formed the beginnings of an idea how he would carry on from there. Indeed, the problems might prove insurmountable without help. And help was something he had no wish to solicit from anyone. The only people who might be prepared to help him would be those who'd also be ready to fight him. Thoughts of which brought his mind to Peter Dimitriu and the old lady.

He knew that the family must have been keeping an eye on him after his acquittal. That was inevitable in the circumstances. What he couldn't know was how far they had been successful. Clearly no expense would have been spared and, even if he had been unable to identify anyone actually on his trail, this was probably no more than a tribute to the skill of those engaged in the task.

Since arriving in Bucharest, he had kept his eyes carefully about him, but had failed to spot any sinister figures lurking behind trees. It had crossed his mind whether

Maricica had been deliberately planted in his path. It was a possibility he couldn't afford to ignore, and, consequently, he'd been careful to give nothing away when they'd been together.

Anyway, he intended taking no chances this evening. Bucharest was a busy, well-thronged city and it wouldn't be difficult to lose himself, particularly after dark. He felt a sharp tingle of excitement. It seemed much more than four months ago that he'd become first involved in the enterprise. More like four decades. Nevertheless, four months into which he had packed a whole life. It was difficult to realise that only ten days before he'd been standing trial for murder. And who knew better than he how close he'd lain to conviction! One false word (he grinned; one true word was, perhaps, the better way of putting it) and he might now be serving a sentence of life imprisonment.

A lot of people had tried to find out exactly what his involvement in the case had been. They had speculated and drawn inferences, while he himself was not without his own areas of speculation. There were things he didn't know or understand and could only guess at. Moreover, they were things which underlined the continuing peril of his position.

Not knowing who was your enemy contributed an eerie element of anxiety. To someone with a stronger imagination than Chris, it would have proved unbearable.

He squirmed into a more comfortable position in bed. It was pleasant to lie there with time no object. But, come to that when had time for him ever been an object? More to the point, would it ever become one? Supposing everything went his way, what was he going to do? It surprised him to realise that he hadn't any idea at all. If you were Chris Laker, you strove towards the goal of making your life easier. But that in itself was meaningless. Did he want a Rolls Royce with a chauffeur? No, he didn't. A country home with servants to wait on him? Not really. Indefinite foreign travel in *de luxe* comfort? For a limited time perhaps, but not for ever. Well, what did he want? For a full minute, he lay staring at the ceiling in contemplation of the question. In the end he decided that all he asked of life was to be a free agent to choose exactly how to spend each day as it came. Yes, he decided, that just about summed it up.

There was a knock on his door and it opened to reveal a

middle-aged female with a broom and a yellow plastic bucket. She laughed at the sight of him in bed, said something which might have been saucy from her expression and closed the door again.

In looks, she reminded Chris slightly of his mother, though in a rather more cheerful edition. It was on his conscience that he had failed to telephone home before leaving. He had promised he would, but, when it came to it, he'd found he couldn't face the unspoken questions and the silent reproach with which he knew he'd be met. It would have been easier, he reflected, if his mother had turned against him . . .

He shifted his position again and this time brought his arm out from beneath the bedclothes to look at his watch. It was just after half past ten.

He'd get up soon and go out. He'd wander about the city looking at some of the advertised sights. The Art Museum, the Patriarchal church, with its curious appearance of clustered pepper-pots, the Athenaeum. These were all places which, the guide-book told him, should be visited by the determined tourist.

Once he left the hotel, he wouldn't return before the evening's undertaking. If anyone was going to try and follow him, they'd better equip themselves with a stout pair of shoes and a packet of sandwiches.

He drew up his knees and kicked off the bedclothes. Slowly he swung his legs over the side and sat up. Then moving across to one end of the window he peered down into the street below. There was certainly no one keeping the hotel under obvious observation, but that didn't mean a thing.

Now, what was that name old Dimitriu had mentioned before his death? It had some vague-sounding connection with an English county. Yes, he'd got it. It was Cornescu. It might be worth remembering if he ran into any trouble.

XVI

Chris let out a stifled oath as he fell heavily on to a spiky root. He got up and rubbed his smarting thigh. He also sucked at a knuckle which was bleeding where a flap of skin had been turned back.

Indeed, his entry into the compound of the Village Museum had taken quite a toll in scratches and minor wrenches. But he was now inside.

He had decided that one of the small picket gates set into the perimeter fence would provide the best place to enter, but this had not turned out to be the case. He had been unable to gain a foothold on the gate and had been obliged to clamber over the fence just to one side of it. What he hadn't reckoned with was the vicious nature of the hedge which reinforced the fence itself. Thank goodness he'd had the foresight to remove his spectacles or they'd certainly have become lost or broken in the course of his exertions.

However, luckily the road outside was both badly lit and quite deserted at two o'clock in the morning, so that the thunderous noises of his entry had failed to attract any attention.

For several minutes, he stood quite still regaining his breath and letting his eyes become accustomed to the dark. Although there was no moon, there was sufficient light to make out shapes and outlines.

With considerable caution he moved forward from the shelter of the bushes among which he had made his inelegant landing. When he broke cover it was to find himself in a farmyard. Happily, one without livestock. Two barns stood silhouetted against the deep mauve sky and he could also see the slender spire of a church off to his left. He remembered the area from his daytime visit. The farm was set at the end of a short track which was a cul de sac.

On reaching the track, he tiptoed across and then paused to take stock on the grass verge of the farther side. He reckoned his objective to be about two hundred yards' distance.

Unfortunately, he couldn't head straight for it, but had to go close to the main entrance where he had noticed, with considerable interest, that there was a small store of labourer's implements stacked in a lean-to shed. Some restoration work had been in progress at one of the cottages which was closed to the public.

He only hoped that they hadn't finished and decamped with their tools.

Flitting from shadow to shadow, he worked his way round to the shed and found to his relief that the implements were still there. He paused for a moment outside and peered intently in the direction of the main entrance, but there was no sign of life. Nevertheless, he hoped the Museum's custodian and his wife, if he had one, were good heavy sleepers.

Armed with a stout shovel, he retraced his steps to the slender-spired church and then set course down the long straight track which, as he recalled, formed the backbone of the Village Museum.

From time to time he paused in the shadow of a tree and listened, but everywhere was still, the only sounds coming from small creatures about their nocturnal business. Once a large bird flew out of a tree, as he approached, with a great flapping of wings. He felt his heart bound into his mouth with the unexpected shock of the commotion and it was half a minute before he was ready to continue.

When he reached the Moldavian farmhouse which was his objective, he passed through the gate almost as though he were arriving back at his own home after several years at sea, save that, for him, there was no time to be lost. This was not a home-coming of relaxed greeting so much as of single-minded rapacity.

Moving out from behind the great cedar tree which dominated the scene, he thrust the spade into the soft earth behind the mossy bank.

For five minutes he dug without interruption, feverishly like a man trying to hide the relics of some dark crime. When he paused to rest, the sweat poured down his body in rivulets which fast turned his clothing into a clinging encumbrance. He removed his jacket and set to again a few yards further on.

It suddenly occurred to him, almost with a feeling of panic, that he could well exhaust himself by his excavations and achieve nothing. What he should have done was prod the earth and only dig when the results of such prodding indicated that it might be profitable to do so.

He cursed himself for not having thought of this before. Why hadn't he given his mind to the physical aspects of the problem? The answer was, he knew, because he was Chris Laker who eschewed the contemplation of such details.

Now, he must go and look for some sort of rod with which to carry out his new idea.

Shoving the spade into the earth, he made his way towards the farmhouse. There was an area at the back where he might find something to suit his purpose. A stout stick might even suffice, but a bit of old railing would be ideal. There must be something of the sort lying about.

But he must hurry. It was nearly three o'clock and, come what may, he'd have to fill in the blasted holes before he left and make sure that all his tracks were covered. He didn't know what time the road outside began to be used in the morning, but he couldn't risk staying a minute after four.

The time element was something else he'd overlooked in his blithe way!

He rounded the corner of the farmhouse when his foot kicked against something. It felt as though it might be what he was looking for. He stooped to pick it up, but got no further.

A pair of arms circled him vice-like from behind and, even before he could react, a pad of chloroform was clamped hard over his nose and mouth.

Great waves of thudding blackness enveloped him until suddenly his conscious mind was snuffed out like a candle.

XVII

When he came to, Chris found he was looking at a dirt-smeared wall which was only a few inches in front of his face.

At first, he was unable to recall what had happened. Indeed, the effort of opening his eyes had made his head feel as though it were occupied by pounding machinery. He closed them again quickly and began to collate the messages which were being laboriously transmitted to his fuddled brain from his extremities.

He was sitting on a chair. Not so much sitting as tied to it. His feet were trussed, as were his hands behind his back. There were also ropes round his body and a gag in his mouth.

Having slowly worked this out, he reopened his eyes, one at a time and with caution, so as not to jar his head. The dirty wall was still there.

Not yet daring to move his head, he rolled his eyes to gain a wider view of the room. There were similar walls on either side about three feet away. The room was suffused with a murky yellow light, presumably from some low-powered bulb out of his vision. There was certainly no daylight in the room, nor any sign of a window. Also the room had a dank smell which made him think he was being held in some basement.

Several minutes went by as he tried unsuccessfully to gather his thoughts on the situation. At least he could now remember being in the Village Museum and going off in search of something with which to prod the ground. He'd been seized from behind and chloroformed.

But by whom? Presumably not anyone connected with the museum. Time would reveal and probably quite soon at that. Meanwhile, he began to experience real fear. Whoever held him captive clearly intended him no good. He was as much at someone's mercy as the next bullock in line for death in the slaughterhouse pen.

Added to his fear was his physical state. He felt that he didn't have a single muscle or limb which wasn't aching or smarting in protest at what had happened to it.

He heard a soft tread behind him and quickly closed his eyes in an ostrich attempt to evade whatever was about to be enacted.

A second later, however, he uttered a stifled cry of pain as someone gave him a vicious flick on his left ear. It was not so much the flick which hurt as the resultant jarring to his whole body with the sharpness of his reaction.

'So you are awake?' a voice said behind him. 'Then we can begin.'

The chair was pulled roughly round, causing him further shooting pains throughout his body.

He'd never seen the man now facing him.

'I think I will leave the gag until we are quite ready.'

Cornescu turned and went out through a narrow door set in a wall which was identical with the others. It was now quite clear that he was being held in a small room in a basement. Over by the door was a trestle table and two wooden chairs. On the table lay the meagre contents of his pockets.

About a couple of minutes went by and then the door opened to admit Cornescu and Peter Dimitriu.

Dimitriu paused on the threshold and gave Chris a long, hard stare of hatred. Chris, for his part, felt a strange upsurge of his spirit. It was the sudden recognition of a familiar face from a more stable era. The absurd illogicality of this only came to him later. The fact that the more stable era was the Old Bailey could hardly have been crazier. Nevertheless, that was his reaction on seeing the tall figure with the fair lank hair and the pale pointed face. Even the hunch of the shoulders brought a touch of reassuring familiarity.

'Shall I remove his gag?' Cornescu asked. Dimitriu nodded in an abstracted way, his eyes still fixed on Chris.

Chris passed his tongue slowly over his bruised and smarting lips. They tasted as if they didn't belong to him. He was aware that Cornescu had remained standing behind him after removing the gag.

'I take it you recognise me?' Dimitriu said coldly.

Chris nodded.

'I'm proposing to ask you some questions and you might as well understand at the outset that I intend to get answers. If necessary, by force.' He took a pace back and leant against the door jamb. 'In case you're wondering where you are and what's happened, let me put your mind at rest about that.' He placed ironic emphasis on the words *at rest*. 'You're still in Bucharest. You haven't been spirited across any frontiers or anything like that. As you've probably guessed, you're in a basement. It's a basement beneath a warehouse. A temporarily disused warehouse.' He glanced round the room like an estate agent before embarking on its qualities. 'The walls are thick and there's no one within a hundred yards of here, anyway. It's as well you should remember that in case you're thinking in terms of cries for help. It also means that if force does have to be used to persuade you to answer my questions, you can shout as loudly as you like. It may help to relieve your feelings, but it won't do anything more than that. Do you understand?'

Chris nodded again.

'Say "yes" then, just to prove that you still have a voice.'

'Yes, I understand.'

'Good, then we're ready to begin. What were you doing in the Village Museum?'

Chris heard Cornescu move slightly behind him and

automatically flinched.

'Don't worry about Ion,' Dimitriu said. 'He's not going to touch you unless you become obstinate.'

Chris had been thinking as rapidly as his battered reflexes permitted. He didn't see that he had any realistic alternative but to answer the questions. In every sense, the game seemed to be up, with the hope of survival all that was left to him. Anyway, if it was Dimitriu and the other man who had caught him in the museum, they must have a fairly good idea what the answer to that first question was.

'Searching for something,' he said.

'What?'

'Gold.'

A sudden light of revelation crossed Dimitriu's face. Chris observed it with surprise. So he hadn't known the answer to his question!

'Gold which my father told you about?'

'Yes.'

'Buried in the Village Museum close to the Moldavian farmhouse?'

'Yes.'

Dimitriu gave a mirthless laugh. 'It's so obvious when one knows,' he said to Cornescu. 'He was born on a farm in Moldavia.' He turned back to Chris.

'How much gold did he tell you was buried there?'

'He didn't say.'

'How much?'

'He didn't . . . ' Chris let out a sharp cry as Cornescu touched the back of his neck with the tip of his burning cigarette.

'About £100,000 worth.'

'What were you to do?'

'Find out if it was still there.'

'And?'

'Report back.'

'And?'

'That was all.'

'What else did he tell you about the gold?'

'That he'd buried it there before fleeing from the country in 1947.'

'What form was it in?'

'Coins.'

There was a silence while Dimitriu nuzzled the back of one of his hands. When he spoke again, his tone was vicious.

'But you were greedy and decided to get the lot for yourself. That's the truth, isn't it? That's why you murdered my father?'

'I didn't murder him.'

Dimitriu stepped suddenly forward and slapped Chris hard across the face. 'You needn't lie to me, you little bastard. I'm not as gullible as an Old Bailey jury.' As he finished speaking, he delivered another stinging slap.

Chris clenched his teeth and shut his eyes. The pain was excruciating and his whole head throbbed as though the blood was trying to burst through all its vessels. When he reopened his eyes, they were watering so that everything was blurred. He observed, however, that Dimitriu was once more leaning against the edge of the door and was watching him.

'That's just a small taste of what's in store for you if you try to get uppish.'

Chris said nothing, but in that moment decided he'd even scores with Dimitriu if he had to follow him round the world to do so. He felt the surge of rage he'd experienced at school when teased about his middle name.

'You and that little lying bitch who perjured herself on your behalf!' Dimitriu said in a savage tone. 'You expect me to listen quietly to your lies after you've murdered my father and got away with it.' Spittle was beginning to form at the corner of his mouth as he went on, 'You don't think I had you kept under surveillance and then followed you across Europe just to be fed lies, do you?' Chris said nothing. 'Well, do you?' Dimitriu moved closer as Chris prepared himself for another blow. It came, this time on the other cheek.

After that Dimitriu's voice seemed to come from a great distance away.

'How did you come to meet my father?'

Chris opened his eyes slowly and pretended not to have heard the question. He reckoned he wasn't far off losing consciousness and hoped that this might come about. Anything to relieve the torment of his body. It was as if his mind had strayed into someone else's tortured body and couldn't get out again.

'I'll ask my question just once more. How did you come to meet my father?'

'Through a . . . through someone.'

'Who?'

'I don't know.'

'His name?'

'I don't know.'

He let out a cry as Cornescu stuck his cigarette once more into the back of his neck and this time held it there for a couple of seconds.

'His name?'

'I honestly don't know. Your father was very secretive . . . '

'Where did you meet this man? I take it it was a man?'

'Yes, it was a man.'

'Where did you meet him?'

'In a pub.'

'Which pub?'

'The Queen's Head in Chelsea.'

'Go on.'

'We just happened to get talking and he asked me if I wanted a job.'

'Yes?'

'And I asked him what sort of a job and . . . ' Chris' eyes slowly closed and he swayed on the chair. 'Everything's going black,' he muttered. 'I can't think . . . I can't see . . . I . . . ' His head fell sideways.

'Is he shamming?' Dimitriu asked impatiently.

'We will soon find out.'

Cornescu took a pin from the lapel of his jacket and jabbed it into Chris' thigh.

Chris felt the sharp prick but had no difficulty in ignoring it. It had been because he reckoned his threshold of pain to have risen so high that he had decided to avoid further questioning – at least for the time being. The unknown man in the pub story was so much cock, but having embarked on it, he found his mind was not sufficiently well functioning to carry it through to a plausible conclusion.

'Get some water,' he heard Dimitriu say. This was followed by footsteps going out of the room. A few minutes later they returned and he braced himself for further punishment.

The force with which the bucketful of water was hurled

into his face knocked his head back and momentarily deprived him of his breath.

Spluttering, he opened his eyes to find both men observing him closely.

'That seems to have done the trick,' Dimitriu said with
grim satisfaction. 'You were telling us about this man you
met in a Chelsea pub who asked if you'd like a job. Remember?'

Chris gazed at him uncomprehendingly.

'Have we got to assist your memory by other means?'

'The gold,' Chris murmured. 'Is it still there?'

'If it is, it's certainly of no further interest to you. Your
days of common thieving are over. Now come back to the
question. I want to know how you got to know my father.'

'Your father?'

'Yes, my father. The man you murdered. I know you had
several meetings with him. How did that come about?'

'He told me about the buried gold.'

'Yes, yes, we've heard that bit.'

'He wanted me to find out if it was still there.'

Contriving to give the impression that his mind had become slightly unhinged, Chris decided that nothing would
move him off the subject of gold. They could ask him what
they liked, but he'd just go on murmuring about the gold,
like the fevered ramblings of a Klondike prospector.

'Why don't we leave him for a bit, Peter. He can't get
away and we have time on our side.'

'Is it all right to leave him tied up like that?'

'Sure.'

'He's not going to flake out and stay flaked out?'

'No. Being tied up like that is not doing his circulation
much good, but he'll be all right. Quite likely he's still feeling
the effects of the chloroform. Come on, Peter. After all,
we've done well. We've found out the most important thing.'

'I dare say, but I've a lot more to learn before I've
finished with the little punk.'

'Sure, sure. Later we'll get the rest out of him.'

Chris had the impression that Dimitriu was reluctant to
break off, but that the other man had lost interest in continuing the interrogation. He wondered what time it was and
how long since they'd knocked him out in the Village
Museum. His body was now racked by one vast ache, but

somehow he must manage to remain conscious. His only chance lay in trying to loosen his bonds after they'd left him. If he couldn't, then it was the end. Trussed, he could only await their further pleasure and there was little doubt what that would ultimaely be.

He didn't imagine that disposal of an unwanted body would prove any more difficult to a resourceful man in Rumania than it would to one in England.

In fact, it would probably be less of a problem here.

XVIII

Detective Chief Inspector Adams had been attending a conference at the Yard. A small-time fence had coughed, as a result of which a vast conspiracy to trade in stolen antique silver had been uncovered. It had ramifications involving several divisions of the M.P.D., including Adams' own manor, and a co-ordinating conference had been called to plan future moves.

The conference over, Adams had planned to slip quietly back to his own headquarters in North London and was consequently dismayed when he received a message to the effect that the Commander, C.I.D. would like to see him before he left.

It was in a distinctly morose frame of mind that he walked down that endless functional corridor and knocked on the door of the Commander's outer office.

'He's free, so I expect he'll see you right away,' said the secretary. 'I think he wants to hear how you're getting on with the Dimitriu case.'

Adams hadn't the slightest doubt that this was so, though confirmation afforded him no comfort. At this moment, he would prefer to talk about almost anything else.

'Ah!' the Commander said as Adams entered. To Adams' sensitive ear it sounded a particularly meaningful exclamation. 'Heard you were in the building and thought I'd like to have a word with you. Especially since you seem to be avoiding me!'

'Avoiding you, sir?'

'It's around two weeks since I gave you the green light to the further Dimitriu inquiries and I thought we'd agreed that you'd keep in touch with me all along the line. But I've not heard so much as a whimper out of you.'

'I'm afraid that's about all you might have heard, sir,' Adams replied.

'Not got very far, have you? I didn't think you would. However, I presume that if you've run into a brick wall, it means you can't have stirred up any nasty smells. Or have you?'

'No, sir, I'm sure I haven't. I mean you've not received any complaints about my further inquiries, have you?'

'Not yet.'

'Well, that's a relief, sir.'

'Stop hedging and relieve yourself a bit more by telling me exactly what you have been up to? For a start, what's Laker been doing since his acquittal?'

'He lay low for about ten days, sir, then he suddenly took off.'

'Took off! Where to?'

'I don't know, sir. He flew to Zurich four days ago, but I'm certain that wasn't his final destination.'

'Why are you certain?'

'I just am, sir.'

'That's not much of a reason. How do you know he hasn't gone to Switzerland for a holiday?'

'Because he'd have taken his girl with him if that had been the case. As it is, he even refused to tell her where he was going. Said it would be safer if she didn't know. Which doesn't make it sound like a holiday!'

'Unless he was off with another bird.'

'I don't think so, sir.'

'All right, so Laker has gone abroad to an unknown country. It doesn't seem to me that the taxpayers need shed too many tears about that.'

'Peter Dimitriu has also gone out of the country,' Adams said bleakly. 'Ostensibly on a journalistic trip to Germany and Switzerland. But I'm pretty sure, sir, that his sudden departure is linked to Laker's.'

'How do you know it's *sudden*?'

'I found out from his secretary that it was a last-minute affair.'

'Couldn't she tell you whether it was a genuine journalistic trip or not?'

'So far as she knew, it was.'

'Well, that's two of them abroad, possibly innocently, possibly not. What else has happened?'

'A third has suddenly flown the ccuntry. Reyman. I heard yesterday. He seems to have departed at even shorter notice than Dimitriu.'

The Commander's mouth twitched in amusement. 'Bloody good show, I'd say. I'm all for their being someone else's problem, particularly if they're bent on mischief. Let's hope they end up behind bars in the prison of a thoroughly putrid county.'

Adams, who didn't share this breezy view, looked glum. 'If that happens, sir, then the mystery surrounding Dimitriu's death will never be solved.'

'You never know, Ted, it might be. If they land themselves in serious trouble, the odds are they'll squeak like hell for the British Consul to come and bail them out and in those sort of circumstances they're much more likely to spill all the beans. If any of them do get lodged in a foreign jail, my bet is that something will come filtering back which'll help to clear up the case.'

'I hope you're right, sir.'

'Quite frankly I don't care whether I am or not. I'm just relieved that they've decided to go and play in someone else's garden. I'm sorry you feel frustrated, but *I'm* a lot happier. I've enough problems without gratuitously inviting others. And that's precisely what I did when I let you go ahead with your further inquiries.'

'But I may still continue?'

'Yes, if there's anyone left for you to interview!' the Commander grinned. 'Incidentally, what had you found out before these boys all trekked off to Heathrow?'

'Nothing specific, sir, but enough to confirm my feeling that we hadn't uncovered half the story.'

'Anything to change your view that Laker did commit the murder?'

Adams shook his head. 'No.'

'You still think he did?'

'Yes, sir.'

'So do I. The pity was we couldn't find more evidence against him. Though people have been convicted on a single fingerprint before now. And, come to that, hanged!'

As Adams drove back to his own headquarters, he wondered whether the Commander's attitude wasn't, perhaps, the saner. Unlike the majority of the police officers, the Commander had never been one to demand his pound of flesh. He'd never felt cheated, either personally or as an official representative of law and order, when a criminal he was after fled the country or committed suicide as sometimes happened.

'Provided he doesn't try and return that suits me,' he'd say. 'It'll also suit the taxpayers.'

Admittedly there were some crimes so heinous that they called out for extradition proceedings. Even the Commander recognised this. But there were far more in which his satisfied cry of 'good riddance' could be properly echoed.

But, reflected Adams, the Commander was exceptional in this respect. It wasn't that he, Adams, thought of himself as vindictive, but he disliked loose ends to a case and it was that which made him still determined to dig out the truth concerning Gheorge Dimitriu's death.

When he arrived in his office, he quickly went through the list of messages awaiting him. There was only one which seized his attention. It read:

'Miss Jane Holland phoned. She will call back between seven and eight. She wouldn't say what it was about, but she sounded excited.'

Adams looked at his watch and saw that the time was now a quarter to seven. He called his wife to say that he wouldn't be home until around half past eight.

Forty minutes later Janey came through.

'I think I've found something important,' she said in a voice tense with anxiety. 'Can you come over?'

'Yes, but tell me first what it is.'

'It's a newspaper cutting. I'm sure it has to do with Chris's disappearance . . . '

'What's the cutting say?' Adams broke in.

'I'd much sooner you saw it. Please come. I'm sure it's a clue.'

Adams gazed into space for a second over the top of the mouthpiece. What was he deliberating for!

'O.K., Miss Holland, I'll be with you in about half an hour.'

There was only one thing he had to do before setting out.

He phoned his wife again, this time to say that he didn't know what time he'd be home.

XIX

Chris wouldn't have believed it possible to have fallen asleep trussed to a chair and with every limb in one's body sending out half-minute protests.

But fall asleep he did after the two men had left him.

When he awoke, it was to feel so awful that he wished he could be knocked out again. His general soreness and stiffness had increased, his head ached dully and his mouth tasted as if it had been scoured with a dirty pot-cleaner. He tried to shift his position on the chair, but succeeded only in almost toppling over.

He wondered whether he had been asleep five minutes or five hours. Not that it mattered, seeing that he had had no idea of the time since he'd been taken by surprise in the Village Museum. The fact that he didn't feel hungry meant nothing and gave no indication of the passage of time. Likewise his intolerable thirst was no guide.

He had been muzzily pondering his situation for about half an hour when he heard soft footsteps outside. The door opened and the man who was not Dimitriu came in, closing the door quietly behind him.

'How are you feeling?' he asked. He spoke quickly and appeared nervous.

'Bloody awful. I want a drink.'

To his surprise, the man disappeared to return a little later with a mug of water, which Chris gulped at greedily when it was held to his mouth.

'Better?'

Chris nodded briefly, his gratitude for the water quickly turning to suspicion. Why was he now being granted favours?

'Dimitriu proposes to kill you,' the man said, watching Chris closely. Chris said nothing, but waited for him to go on. 'I do not like to see a man killed in cold blood.' Still Chris said nothing. 'Anyway, I do not agree that he should kill you *here*.' Chris was unsure whether he was referring to Rumania, Bucharest or the actual basement in which he was being held prisoner. Whichever it was, he shared the sentiment. 'He will be coming back soon to ask you more questions. And after that he will kill you for having murdered his father. By the way, I have not introduced myself. I am Cornescu. Ah, I see from your expression that you have heard of me.'

'Yes.'

'I have known the Dimitriu family very long time, but I still do not think it right you should be killed like Christmas goose.' He smiled faintly. 'You should be like the partridge and have a chance to live. That is why I will help you.'

'How?'

'I will make it possible for you to free yourself. If you succeed, you may be able to avoid death.'

'What time is Dimitriu coming back?'

'In one hour, perhaps. He will find you still here, but if you try hard enough, you should have got free by then.'

'What's to prevent my getting free before he comes back and making my escape?'

Cornescu made a face of Gallic deprecation. 'I shall not make it *so* easy for you. Also the door will be locked. And it is a strong lock.' He glanced at his watch. 'And now I give you help.'

He moved behind the chair and Chris felt him pulling at rope which bound his hands. For a couple of minutes he worked away while Chris tried to assess exactly what he was doing. Then he stepped back in front of the chair and said:

'There!'

One hand, his left, was firmly tied to the back of the chair, but the other was now free. Slowly, painfully, Chris brought it round and rested the hand on his lap, gazing at it as if it were some small injured creature he'd just rescued.

Cornescu leant forward and seized the hand, vigorously massaging the wrist which bore deep weals where the rope had chafed and bitten into the flesh. Chris winced with pain.

'And now, my friend, it is up to you,' he said, moving towards the door.

'What time is it? You can at least tell me that before you go.'

'It is four o'clock on the afternoon of Wednesday.'

A second later he had gone, leaving Chris to contemplate his new situation. For several minutes, he sat quite still, apart from slowly flexing the fingers of his freed hand, which felt as if they were filled with hundreds of small needles.

The it came to him with a rush of realisation that this was no time to ponder Cornescu's curious behaviour. Immediate action was required. There'd be time to work out whys and wherefores later – if he was lucky. And his luck was going to depend on how quickly he was able to free himself.

Ignoring the sharp jab of pain in his shoulder, he brought his arm right across his body and felt for the end of the rope which bound his other wrist. It was just within reach of his fingers and he feverishly began to pluck at it.

He was coming close to despair, when the knot which had seemed to be cemented in place suddenly yielded a fraction to his efforts. One strand came loose, but it was sufficient to send his hopes soaring.

Twenty minutes later, his left hand was free and he was able to turn his attention to the rope which bound his ankles together and fettered his legs to the chair. Though he now had both hands to work with, the effort was no less, largely because of the strain of bending down. But at last they too, were released and the rope lay discarded on the floor. Very gingerly he stood up and with equal caution took a step forward, quickly reaching for the chair as he felt himself about to pitch forward.

Holding on to the top of the chair, be began again, using it as a support. He remembered having seen a documentary film of disabled people learning to walk with the similar aid of a chair.

After a few minutes, he decided, once more, to try and go solo and this time managed to cross the room without disaster.

Satisfied that he could now both stand and walk without toppling over, he put himself through a few elementary exercises, at the end of which he decided he was in better shape than he'd have imagined. God knows, he still ached in every limb of his body, but he was alive and vigorously determined to stay that way.

He was still practising various movements when he became aware of approaching footsteps.

Kicking the rope under the table, he quickly sat down on the chair and held his hands behind his back. Whoever it was, he'd rush him as soon as the door opened.

He heard the key turn in the lock and the next moment Peter Dimitriu came into the room.

Chris hurled himself out of the chair straight at his adversary. Caught completely off balance, Dimitriu reeled back under the onslaught and thudded against the passage wall outside, with Chris clutching the lapels of his jacket.

Chris was aware of an expression of demonic fury seizing Dimitriu's face. Drawing back his arm, he aimed a blow at the face with all the strength he could muster. He grunted with pain as his fist skidded off the top of Dimitriu's shoulder and cracked into the wall. At the same moment, Dimitriu brought his knee hard up into Chris' groin. But Chris had realised what was coming and done a quick side movement so that the knee connected only with his thigh. Seizing the raised leg, he gave it a tremendous jerk to try and unfoot the other man, but, with the support of the wall behind him, Dimitriu managed to frustrate the attempt and a second later they had shot back through the door, this time with Chris on the receiving end of the assault. He crashed backwards into the chair, overbalanced and fell with Dimitriu on top of him.

For a couple of minutes, they rolled locked together on the floor, grunting, panting, and working all the while for an opening to seize the initiative.

Dimitriu freed one of his hands and made a grab at Chris' face, fingers curled like talons. Chris threw back his head, then brought it forward and fastened his teeth on two of the questing fingers. He bit as hard as he could until he tasted blood. Dimitriu yelped with pain as he tried to release the fingers, but Chris held on even though his front teeth felt as though they were about to be wrenched out. Then abruptly he opened his mouth and in that second in which the initiative passed to him, he thrust himself on top of Dimitriu and seizing his head in both hands banged it as hard as he could on the stone floor. Not once, but in a series of dull thumps until the man's whole body went limp, his eyes rolled back and a dribble of blood came from one nostril.

Trembling violently all over, Chris got to his feet, only

to stagger across to the chair and sit down. It was several minutes before he trusted himself to stand up, during which time Dimitriu lay unconscious, his face the same colour as his flaxen hair. He was breathing heavily so that when he exhaled his whole body appeared to shudder.

Going across to the table, Chris put on his spectacles and pocketed his possessions which were lying there. Then without giving Dimitriu another look he stepped out into the passage and locked the door behind him, throwing the key as far as he could into the cavernous darkness which swallowed up the passage in one direction.

Setting off in the other he came to a flight of stairs which he cautiously mounted, after first pausing to listen for any sounds. But he could hear nothing save the thumping of his own heart.

The staircase doubled back on itself and Chris found himself coming up into what appeared to be an empty warehouse. Such light as there was filtered through two begrimed skylights at either end. The floor was broken up and littered with rubbish.

There were high double doors not far from the top of the staircase and Chris tiptoed across to examine them. The need for complete quietness was uppermost in his mind. He must get out of the place without being seen or heard, at all costs.

He had just begun to run his hands over the door when a car roared to a halt outside and somebody jumped out and began beating on the door with his hands. Chris leapt back in alarm and ran to the farther end of the warehouse.

Behind a stack of old furniture he came across a small door which, miracle of miracles, opened at his touch. He was in a narrow blind alley running up to the street in which the car had stopped. Ten paces brought him to the edge of the pavement and with great caution he peeped round the corner.

The street appeared to be deserted apart from the car twenty yards down and two men who were trying to force the warehouse door with their shoulders.

It didn't require a second glance to see that they were police.

As Chris quickly withdrew his head there was a sound of

splintering wood and when he peered again, only the car remained in sight.

In a flash he had set off along the street in the opposite direction. It joined a lateral road about fifty yards down and he turned right and slowed down, for this was a fairly busy thoroughfare with people strolling along the pavements and looking into shop windows. He reckoned he must appear bizarre enough anyway without drawing further attention to himself by charging down the street like an escaped bullock.

Luckily, he hadn't gone far before he came upon a taxi. He climbed in before the driver realised what was happening and murmured, 'Hotel Apollo.'

The driver turned his head and stared at him without pleasure. He said something which Chris didn't understand, but made no effort to drive off.

'Hotel Apollo,' Chris repeated.

The driver repeated his observation.

Impasse appeared to have been reached and Chris was experiencing mounting panic when a sudden thought struck him. Reaching for his wallet he pulled out a one-hundred-lei note and waved it under the driver's nose, whereupon the man gave him a sly wink and started up the engine.

It took them about ten minutes to reach the hotel. The lobby was empty and Chris charged straight across and up the stairs. He had reached his floor before realising that he hadn't collected his key. But perhaps the door would be unlocked. He'd noticed that the staff weren't very punctilious about relocking doors after they'd been in. His one idea was to collect his belongings and get out. He had no clear idea of what he was going to do then, but instinct told him to cut loose from the hotel without delay. If anyone was on his tracks, that was where they'd look for him.

He reached his room and turned the handle. To his infinite relief, the door opened.

As it did so, there was a small cry of alarm from inside the room and he found himself face to face with Maricica, who was standing over by his suitcase, which lay open.

XX

Janey opened the door as soon as Adams knocked. She left him to close it behind him and went across to the dressing-table by the window.

'I found this,' she said, holding out a newspaper cutting in her hand. 'It was in Chris' copy of *The Catcher in the Rye*. He was re-reading it after his trial.' She picked up the Penguin edition of the book as though to prove the truth of what she was saying.

Adams took the cutting from her and slowly read it. It ran:

'Young man with sense of adventure wanted for one month's work involving some travel. All expenses and extravagant remuneration for the successful applicant. Reply, stating age and physical particulars (height, weight, etc.) to Box 2306.'

'What paper did your young man usually read?' he asked, looking up.

'The *Daily Telegraph*, for the ads. He was always on the look-out for something like that.'

'And you think this was the start of everything?' He flicked at the cutting with a finger-nail.

She nodded. 'I'm sure it's a clue. I'm so worried about him, Mr Adams. Please do what you can.'

'The first thing is to find out when this appeared. That shouldn't prove too difficult. Whether or not the paper'll be able to tell us who inserted it remains to be seen.'

Secretly, Adams was as excited about the cutting as Janey was, if for different reasons. For him, it could be a clue to the truth. Its ultimate effect on the fate of Master Laker was a matter of complete indifference to him. He didn't mind if he never saw him again. Indeed, he rather hoped he wouldn't, for if this cutting did have any relevance it would be to prove a link between accused and deceased. An evidential link which must surely have led to Laker's conviction if the prosecution had known of it in time. But to come into possession of further evidence now would be additionally galling if Laker himself was around to add salt to the wound.

148

To Janey who was watching him expectantly, he forbore to point out that her find might go to prove what he had all along suspected, namely that she'd committed perjury. There'd be time enough to deal with that situation when he'd made the further investigation.

He slipped the cutting into his notebook which he returned to his pocket.

'You've not heard anything from him?'

'No. It's so worrying.'

'Look, Janey, why don't you forget him. He's brought you a good deal of unhappiness already and you can take it from me, that's only the beginning if you stick by him. You could find somebody better.'

'I don't want anyone better.'

Adams shrugged. 'Well, it's your life, but it seems to me a pity to tie your fortunes to that young man. I know all about what the love of a good woman is supposed to be able to achieve, but your work's going to be cut out with him.'

'I thought you were on my side now,' she said in a voice both angry and bitter.

'It sounds smug, but I'm only interested in finding out the truth.'

'The truth as you want it to be!'

'No, the truth.' He gave her a faint smile and, patting his pocket, said, 'And I think you may have brought me closer to it by finding that cutting.'

To himself, as he went downstairs, he added, 'I just hope the truth won't hurt you more than all the lying has so far.'

XXI

Large men are often patient men, being endowed with apparently inexhaustible supplies of that well vaunted quality, denied their smaller and frequently tetchier brethren. It was certainly so in Alex Reyman's case, which was just as well seeing that he had been forced to spend his first day in Bucharest tailing Chris, whom he had got on to easily enough by first tailing Cornescu.

It had become apparent to him quite early on that Chris was killing time – he couldn't possibly have any real in-

terest in the various museums and churches he chose to visit
– but there was no knowing when he wouldn't suddenly
take off.

By mid-afternoon Reyman had come to the conclusion
that nothing was likely to happen before nightfall.

He had followed Chris out to the Village Museum in his
hired Simca and from a safe position had seen him climb
over the fence into the park.

This, apart from pin-pointing his actual interest inside,
had told him what he needed to know.

He'd been certain for a long time that the old man had
left something hidden, buried in his homeland. Something
which he'd been unable to take with him when he fled. It
was obviously something valuable and it was a reasonable
guess that it was something unmanageably heavy. Reyman
reckoned it must be either gold or jewellery. Anway, whatever it was was presumably hidden within the confines of the
Village Museum – or had been.

He'd been about to drive off when he'd noticed Cornescu's
car parked beneath a tree on the road which ran
along another side of the park. Intrigued, he had stopped
and waited.

It had not been his intention to follow Chris into the park,
anyway. Tomorrow in daylight would be soon enough to
make his own reconnaissance.

In all he had waited over an hour, but he had been re-
warded by seeing Dimitriu and Cornescu emerge through
one of the wicket gates carrying an inert body between them.

He wondered how they'd come by a key to open the gate
and decided that the lock had been picked. He recalled how
Cornescu, the only time he'd met him on his visit to London,
had spent an inordinate time gazing at Chubb's window
in St James's Street and had explained that he was fascinated
by the mechanism of all locks.

When the car bearing Chris, Dimitriu and Cornescu had
driven off, he'd not followed it since this would have been
taking an unnecessary risk at such an hour of the morning
when the streets were virtually empty of traffic.

He assumed that Chris would be taken back to Cornescu's
flat. Not that it bothered him where he was taken. He
regarded himself as being in the happy position of seeing
his opponents metaphorically knocking each other out –

literally, too, in the case of Chris. All he had to do was wait, watch and then time his own swoop on the scene.

He'd gone to bed well satisfied.

The next day – or rather at a more civilised hour of the same morning he went out to the Village Museum as an ordinary tourist and strolled around, though with anything but an ordinary tourist's eye.

He had somehow expected to find signs of last night's intrusion, but there were none. Moreover, the museum staff gave no indication that anything untoward had taken place.

He was surprised and also irked, for he'd been sure that something would strike his determinedly observant eye. Moreover, he had entered every cottage, shed and house in his search for a clue.

At the Moldavian farmhouse, he had seen a bed of newly dug earth and was speculatively looking at it, when the guide had come up and said that some very beautiful flowers were about to be planted. Reyman was not to know that he was doing no more than offering a glib answer to an unasked question, a practice not unknown to guides.

At all events, he'd left the museum considerably disgruntled and, after a quick lunch, had gone off to where Cornescu lived. From a public telephone farther down the street, he called Cornescu's number. He was fairly certain that it was Dimitriu who answered. He asked to speak to a Herr Schuette, using German which was the only foreign tongue he knew. Then apologising for having obtained a wrong number, he'd quickly rung off. He'd confirmed that someone was in the flat, which was what he'd wanted to find out.

About three-quarters of an hour later, he saw Cornescu leave the building and get into his car. He followed him in his hired one at a discreet distance.

Eventually, Cornescu parked outside a warehouse and unlocking a side door, entered. Reyman moved his own car to a vantage point and kept watch.

It was about half an hour before Cornescu reappeared and he was particularly interested to observe that he didn't appear to lock the door behind him on leaving.

He let Cornescu drive off and then retired to a nearby café to think things over. The upshot was that he decided to have a look round the warehouse himself.

It was while he was doing this that he had heard dull thudding sounds from somewhere in the basement.

He'd been about to creep down and see what was happening when he'd heard footsteps on the stairs and had quickly withdrawn behind an insecure pyramid of old packing-cases. Consequently he'd not seen who it was leaving.

By now he was thoroughly intrigued and had come round to wondering whether this mightn't be the focal point of his interest. Could it be that old Dimitriu's hidden haul had already been brought here!

He was moving stealthily along the basement passage and had just reached the door of Chris' cell when he was startled by a rush of footsteps on the stairs and turned to find himself confronted by two rapidly approaching police officers with drawn pistols.

They had no need to say anything. Their meaning was clear.

XXII

Maricica's hand shot up to her mouth in classic gesture, and she blinked as though unable to believe her eyes.

'I know I look a sight,' Chris remarked in a not too friendly tone, 'but I gather it's more than that which has surprised you.'

'I do not understand . . . ' she murmured hesitantly.

'Let's see if we can sort this out; but quickly. You obviously weren't expecting to see me, but what are you doing in my room?'

She was still gaping at him and seemed to be transfixed with fear.

'I was looking for . . . ' She broke off. 'I was told you were in prison, that is why I am surprised to see you.'

'That makes sense! But who told you I was in prison?'

'Ion Cornescu.'

'So he's a friend of *yours*, too, is he?'

I can explain everything,' she said, miserably.

'That would be a good idea! You do some explaining while I do some packing.'

'Cornescu paid me to meet you at the airport and bring

you to this hotel, where the proprietor is a friend of his.'

'So you're not in the travel agency business?'

She hung her head. 'No.'

'What else did Cornescu pay you to do?' he asked in a tone which made her wince.

'Nothing. I promise.'

'What did he tell you about me?'

'Just that you had done much harm to the family of the other man – the man from England and were still trying to cheat them.'

'That all?'

'Yes.'

'Did he tell you anything about a murder trial?'

'No,' she said in a puzzled tone.

'You know what I mean by "murder trial"?'

'Yes. A court affair.'

'He didn't tell you anything about that?'

'No, definitely not.'

'Was it Cornescu's idea that you spent an evening with me?'

'No, it was mine, because I liked you.'

'Let's get back to the present. What were you looking for here?'

She blushed and appeared to be on the verge of tears.

'Money. English money.'

'What do you want English money for?'

'I can explain.'

'Go ahead, I'm listening.'

'For meeting you at the airport and bringing you to this hotel, the other man was going to deposit money in Paris for me. We cannot take money with us from Rumania, but we can travel if there is money when we get there. I have always longed to go to Paris. That was to be my payment.'

'Now tell me what Cornescu said about my being in prison?'

'He told me only an hour ago. He said you and the other Englishman had been involved in a fight and that the police had arrested you.'

'The sly bastard!' Chris exclaimed with feeling. 'Then it must have been he who sent the police round to the warehouse. Of all the mean, rotten, underhand tricks!' Maricica gazed at him in alarm as the words were spat out. 'So seeing your trip to Paris up the spout,' he went on, 'you were looking round for alternative means of support?'

'I am sorry, but I do not understand what you say.'

'Skip it.' He closed his suitcase and lifted it off the bed. Then going across to the wash-basin he sloshed water all over his face and put a comb through his hair. He grimaced at his reflection in the mirror. Unshaven, face the colour of boiled silverside, swollen from Dimitriu's blows, and enough scratches to make it appear he'd been making love to a coil of barbed wire. 'Right, I'm ready. I'm paying the bill and checking out, and you're coming with me.'

She followed him submissively out of the room. It occurred to him as they went downstairs that they were rather like a couple of poker players who didn't hold a royal card between them; though, at the moment, Maricica was unaware of this.

Outside on the pavement, he said, 'Let's go to a quiet café where we can talk.'

When they were seated and he had ordered a tuica for Maricica and a beer for himself, he said, 'I've got to get out of Rumania quickly and you're going to help me.'

'But how can I help you?'

'I'll tell you. I have my return ticket, so all I need to do is book a flight. You're going to do that for me and you're also going to smooth over any difficulties for me at the airport. You did so on my arrival, and you can jolly well give a repeat performance on my departure.' He paused and gave her a speculative look. 'I realise you're a commercially minded girl, and that I mustn't expect you to help me for nothing. So here's the proposition. Provided I get safely back to England, I'll see that there's money for your trip to Paris. O.K.?'

She bit her lip and shook her head slowly as though unable to comprehend the bargain he was suggesting.

'I am very sorry,' she said in such a quiet voice that Chris could only just hear what she said.

'You mean you don't agree?'

'I am very sorry that I was trying to steal from you.'

'Forget that. I'd have done the same in the circumstances. You've been let down and I'm in a jam, partly of my own making, partly not. But I needn't bother you with the details of that. The thing is that I must get on the first available plane. I suggest we go out to the airport straight away and see if there's one anywhere this evening. Drink up and we'll get a taxi.'

They hardly spoke on their way out to the airport, but once Maricica slipped her hand into his and squeezed it. Just before they arrived, he began to say something, but she stopped him with a gesture.

'The driver might have understood some English,' she explained after they had got out.

He glanced anxiously around him, but everything appeared to be normal. There were certainly no signs of police activity.

Leaving him on the steps of the building outside, Maricica hurried in with his ticket.

It seemed to Chris that she was away for ages. Indeed, he even began to wonder if he hadn't been crazily trusting to part with his ticket. Supposing she used it to fly off herself. He broke out into a sweat at the thought and peered anxiously through the glass doors into the brightly lit interior. Then he saw her over at one of the counters on the far side. It was another ten minutes, however, before she rejoined him.

'There is a plane to Vienna in one hour.'

'That's a bit of luck,' he remarked.

'You will have to wait in Vienna for a plane to London tomorrow.'

'I'll stay there till next year if I have to.'

'I told them,' she went on, 'that you had to return to England in a hurry because your mother is very sick.'

'It might even be true,' he said cheerfully, but checked himself when he noticed her expression of faint disapproval. 'What shall we do for the next hour?' he asked quickly. 'What can one do at airports other than drink?'

The bar was full of Bucharest citizens sharing the vicarious pleasures of travel and the place rang with cheerful noise.

Chris ordered a tuica for each of them and raised his glass in a silent toast, his lips framing the words, 'To Paris.'

Maricica, however, was clearly nervous and Chris whose own emotions were fluctuating wildly began fidgeting so badly that he had to go outside for fear he drew attention to himself.

It was a relief to each of them when the Vienna flight was called.

Maricica accompanied him as far as she could. He bent and kissed her on the mouth and, with a little wave, turned to pass through immigration control.

A minute later he was in the departure lounge awaiting the call to board the plane. His passport had been stamped after no more than a cursory glance, while he himself had been subjected to nothing worse.

As he stood in the lounge and looked back, he could see Maricica still standing where he'd left her, only fifteen yards and two glass doors away. But he felt as though they were separated by a whole firmament.

Not until the plane was airborne did he relax.

He couldn't think how he'd been able to get away so easily, but it must have been touch and go.

It was no good trying to analyse your luck, you just accepted it. And on the whole, he'd always been lucky. Well, almost always!

XXIII

Mrs Dimitriu was worried. More worried than she cared to acknowledge. Her son had promised to call her the previous evening and had failed to do so. She had eventually tried to contact him at Cornescu's number, but had received no answer. She had gone on trying, as well as again this morning, but without result.

She was desperately afraid that something had gone wrong and dreaded to contemplate what it might be. Peter was all that mattered to her. All that ever *had* mattered to her.

He'd been so certain that he could handle the situation with Cornescu's aid and she had fully supported him in the decision to follow Laker to Bucharest. Indeed, it had been her idea, her mind still obsessed with discovering the truth surrounding her husband's death, and her son had readily agreed.

For the first time since a serious illness several years back, she suddenly felt as if she were an old woman. Too many of her props had been snatched away too abruptly. The sense

156

of terrifying drift she was beginning to experience would seize her like a fever if anything had happened to Peter.

She walked over and examined herself in a wall mirror. Certainly no one would guess she was verging on panic. Her features were still set in their familiar mould of haughty disdain and her inner feelings were completely concealed.

Moving out on to the terrace, she gazed with a disenchanted eye at the small walled garden that was laid out with the precision of a mosaic. Only the two goldfish endlessly circling in the tiny lily pond did anything to disturb the impression of unnatural order. It was impossible to think of plants growing in such a garden. They were just there.

Anyway, the garden meant nothing to her. It was merely somewhere to sit on the rare days when the sun shone hotly as it used to in her native Rumania during the summer.

She gave a little shiver and turned back into the room. She knew she should try and occupy her mind with things to do. She was a superb cook and enjoyed practising the higher culinary arts, so why didn't she go into the kitchen and concoct some delicious dish. But the idea was only conceived to be brusquely dismissed.

She sat down and stared at the large open fireplace which was filled with a bank of fir cones she had painted black and white.

Her mind went over the last few years of her married life. She tried to identify the moment she first became aware that they'd drifted apart and decided that it had been a long, slow process which had probably begun with Peter's birth.

It was only during the past two years that he had begun to behave in such an obviously secretive way. He had never been given to taking her into his confidence about his business affairs and she had never bothered to pry. It was a fact, however, that latterly he had become even less communicative.

Within the last two or three months of his life, he had started to behave most strangely, going out at unaccustomed times without saying a word and coming home at all hours without a murmur of an explanation.

What was he up to? she and Peter had wondered. This was the question which had gnawed ceaselessly at her mind – and continued still to do so.

It had naturally come as a great shock to learn that his

estate was only a fraction of the expected amount. And the baffling part was that no one had any idea where it had all gone. It was now apparent that he'd realised a very large part of his holding of securities, but the money had vanished. Nearly half a million pounds had slipped unnoticed away. But where to?

And what about the young man, Laker? He was obviously in it up to his neck, but how had he come to be involved with her husband? These were questions which had tormented her mind during every waking hour. They were questions without answers, hence Peter's dramatic journey to Bucharest.

She'd always known that her husband maintained one or two vague ties with his homeland, that he had occasional business dealings with Cornescu, for example, but that was all. Could it be that his secretly disposed assets had found their way there? It would account for Laker's sudden departure for that country.

She looked across at the silent telephone and willed it to ring. But it remained stubbornly inanimate. In a sudden impulse, she got up and went over and dialled a number.

'I'd like to speak to Mr Reyman,' she said when someone answered.

'I'm afraid he's not here.'

'When will he be back please?'

'He didn't say how long he'd be away.'

'May I ask where he's gone?'

'Abroad.'

She dropped the receiver as though it had stung her. So, he'd gone abroad, too! She could guess where. Trust Alex Reyman to be after some imagined juicy pickings!

She had never liked him and had never trusted him. From one or two things Gheorge had let drop a year or so back, she'd inferred that he'd been caught out trying to cheat his employer. For all she knew, he'd later succeeded. That wouldn't surprise her in the slightest, astute though she knew her husband to have been. She couldn't understand why he'd been kept on. Presumably, his uses outweighted his deficiencies. There was no other explanation.

A sudden savage thought flared through her mind. If Reyman was in any way responsible for landing Peter in serious trouble, she'd hunt him down and kill him herself.

158

The day passed in growing anxiety, fuelled by the hours of sterile inactivity.

It was around seven o'clock in the evening that she received a terse message, via the police, to the effect that one Peter Dimitriu had been found dead of head injuries in Bucharest and that an Englishman was being held for questioning.

As the telephone receiver dropped from her hand, she let out a terrible, convulsing moan and pitched to the floor in a faint.

XXIV

Detective Chief Inspector Adams heard the news at about the same time.

He was in the station canteen on his second pint of beer when the phone rang and the P.C. who had answered it shouted out across the not inconsiderable din, 'It's for you, sir,' at the same time stabbing the air in Adams' direction.

'Can't even drink in peace these days,' he grumbled to Detective Sergeant Paget as he put down his tankard and got up.

'When could you ever in the canteen!' Paget observed.

When Adams returned to the table, he said, 'That was a message about Peter Dimitriu. He's been found dead in Bucharest.'

'I thought he'd gone to Rumania.'

'Bucharest is Rumania.'

'I thought it was Hungary.'

'That's Budapest.'

'Oh! Daft having two places with similar names like that! Anyway, what'd he die of?'

'Head injuries. The police are holding someone for questioning. An Englishman.'

'Laker?'

'The message didn't say. Some of it got lost in transmission. I've told them to find out and call back. I presume it's Laker – or Reyman.'

'Either way, it's someone else's problem and I'm all for that.'

159

'If it's Laker, it removes our last chance of ever discovering the truth.'

Sergeant Paget, who had a less curious mind and who generally opted for life's short cuts, shrugged. 'I'd call it poetic justice. He slithered out here, but has collected his greens in someone else's country.'

'If it is Laker,' Adams added.

Half an hour later he was called to the phone again and returned to announce:

'It's Reyman they're holding.'

Sergeant Paget absorbed this piece of news in silence for a moment, then asked. 'Any news of Laker?'

'No.'

'Pity the Rumanian police haven't got him, too.' But Adams wasn't listening. 'With any luck he'll be back in England quite soon,' he said aloud, though more to himself than to his companion.

'He's had a darned sight too much luck, if you ask me.'

Adams glanced up sharply. 'I'm not thinking of his, I'm thinking of mine. Where there's Laker, there's hope. Hope that the day will dawn when there's nothing left for me to find out about the Dimitriu case.'

'Some hope!'

'You can go and buy us both another pint of beer and we'll drink to it whether you want to or not.'

Sergeant Paget grinned and departed with their empty tankards. You had to hand it to the Chief Inspector, he was a real terrier. Whereas he, Sergeant Paget, was more like one of those large, ambling dogs who'd merely stare incuriously if a rabbit ran under their nose.

'O.K., sir,' he said on his return, 'here's to hope, and you buy the next pint.'

XXV

Janey had felt low ever since Chief Inspector Adams' visit. He had left her demoralised and far from sure that she'd done the right thing in showing him the cutting. He had arrived as a friend and departed as a sort of unwelcome angel of righteousness.

Her sense of anxiety and depression had reflected itself

in her work, and her boss, who'd already had his patience worn thin as a result of the Old Bailey business, had snapped at her, which had promptly reduced her to tears. He had then gruffly suggested that she should go home and she had retorted, through sniffs, that on the contrary she would stay late in order to get abreast of the work. He had accepted this gesture without enthusiasm which had sent her morale down a further couple of pegs.

However, the upshot was that it was eight o'clock before she let herself into the house that evening. She had bought a single sausage roll for her supper on her way home and then eaten it in the Tube because she couldn't be bothered to carry it in its silly little paper-bag. It had tasted stale and clammily cold, which matched her mood.

She reached the landing and inserted the key in the lock of her door. A second later she was staring in wild disbelief at Chris' sleeping form on the bed.

Her eyes prickled with tears and a great lump formed in her throat as she stood rooted to the floor looking at him. Then slowly she tiptoed round to the further side of the bed and with tears of inexpressible joy and relief, she bent down and gently kissed him on the temple.

He sat up with a start.

'Hey, you're all wet! Is it raining?'

'Oh, Chris!' She flung herself into his arms where she broke into sobs, so that it was several minutes before they attempted speech.

'Oh, Chris, how wonderful that you're back,' she said at last through her tears. She disengaged her head from his shoulder and studied him. 'But you've been hurt! What's happened and where've you been?' She stopped abruptly. 'I'm not asking questions, I just want to know you're all right.'

He gave her a funny little smile.

'I don't mind if you do ask questions.'

'I don't want to ask questions. It's none of my business.'

'My poor Janey!' he murmured, pulling her head towards him and kissing her warmly on the lips.

'When did you get back?' she asked when the kiss was over. 'Oh, there, I've asked another question and I didn't mean to.'

'You're obviously as full of questions as a baby is of wind, so I'll give you some answers. I got back about three hours ago. I've been in Rumania and I'm all right; but only just. Now it's my turn to ask you one. Has anyone been inquiring after me while I've been away?'

'Chief Inspector Adams has. He wanted to know where you'd gone. And I was able to tell him I didn't know,' she added with almost a touch of pride. Her expression clouded over. 'He was here two nights ago.'

'What did he want this time?'

She bit her lip. 'I was so worried about you, I was almost out of my mind and I thought he might be able to help . . . to help find you and see that everything was all right. I'd found that cutting, you see. It was in *The Catcher in the Rye* and I gave it to him. I thought it would help him to discover where you were, so that if you were in any danger he'd be able to help . . . ' She broke off miserably, aware that her explanations might sound like confessions of high treason to Chris.

All he said, however, was, 'Funny, I thought I'd destroyed it. The cutting, I mean, not the book.'

'It *was* connected with everything that's happened, wasn't it?' she asked in a small voice.

He nodded. 'It was the start of the whole lark. I answered it and as a result I met old Gheorge Dimitriu. We met three times in all. He used to pick me up at Turnpike Lane Underground Station and we'd drive out to some quiet spot. The first time, he just asked me a mass of questions about myself. At the end he gave me £10 and arranged to meet me again the following week. On that occasion he asked me a lot more questions and told me a bit about himself. On the third he told me how he'd buried a box of gold coins in a park in Bucharest before he'd had to flee his country, and he wanted to find out if they were still there. He said he didn't want his family to know anything about it and there was no one he could trust, so that was why he'd put the advertisement in the paper. He said all I had to do was find out if the gold was still there and he would then make arrangements to get it out. If it was, he was going to give me £5,000, but even if it weren't he'd still give me £1,500. Also he gave me £10 every time we met.

'Anyway, that was the third meeting and he told me that at the next he would give me final instructions, including the exact location of the buried gold.' Chris paused. 'If I'd known it was going to land me in one-quarter of the trouble it has I wouldn't have done it for twice the money.'

'Why did he want to discover whether the gold was still there?'

'He didn't go into all the details, but I gathered he wanted to set up a foundation for political refugees in Switzerland. It was to be called the Dimitriu Foundation. He'd been secretly channelling money over there for some time and wanted to put the gold to the same purpose if he could get hold of it. But he was very anxious that nothing should leak out about the Foundation until he was ready to announce its establishment. He told me his family knew nothing and, in fact, I was the only person to whom he'd revealed his great dream.' He paused and stared abstractedly across the room. 'He was a funny old boy. I think he took quite a fancy to me in his own curious way.' Chris smiled wryly. 'Anyway, you can see what my chances at the Old Bailey would have been if the police had found all that out!'

Janey put up a hand and gently touched his cheek. In a voice which was scarcely above a whisper, she said, 'But it wasn't you who murdered him, was it?'

'No. But nobody was going to believe me if I'd told the truth.'

'Who did do it?'

He gazed straight into her eyes for several seconds, then shook his head. 'I don't know.'

XXVI

Detective Chief Inspector Adams bunched himself for a quick exit as soon as the car stopped. At the sight of him, Sergeant Paget had an insane desire to accelerate away from the kerb.

Instead, he said reprovingly, 'Even if he *is* back, they'll most likely be in bed and ...'

'If he's back,' Adams broke in, 'I don't mind what he's doing, I'm going to talk to him tonight.'

Before Paget had time to get out of the driver's seat, his superior officer was hammering on the front door. Once inside he mounted the stairs with the ungainliness of an eager bulldog while Paget trailed behind in more decorous ascent.

Arriving outside Janey's door he gave it three fierce raps. From inside came sounds of vague stirrings and shortly afterwards the catch was slipped and Chris' tousled head appeared round the edge of the door.

'Ah! So you *are* back,' Adams exclaimed with satisfaction, as he pushed his way into the room.

Janey was sitting up in bed, looking scared and holding a sheet in front of her.

'We'll wait outside while you put some clothes on,' Adams said breezily. 'No need to dress up, I'm not taking you off to the station.'

When they re-entered the room a couple of minutes later, Janey was encased in a long house-coat and Chris was wearing a rather more exiguous garment that revealed most of his chest and all his legs.

'Sorry to come barging in like this,' Adams said in a tone which belied his words, 'but I wanted to make sure of catching you before you disappeared again. Mind if I sit down?' He pulled up a chair from which he removed Chris' clothes, casting them on to the bed. As though to dissociate himself from the intrusion, Sergeant Paget went and stood by the door.

'Now let's begin,' Adams went on. 'The sooner we do, the sooner we end.' He spoke with the revival of vigour of one who at long last thinks he sees the finishing post. 'Am I correct in thinking you're just back from Rumania?'

'Yes.'

'Care to tell me why you went there?'

'I don't mind telling you,' Chris said, as he began to pick his wary way through recent events while Adams and Paget listened impassively.

When he had finished, Adams grinned wolfishly. 'So you still don't know whether, in fact, the gold exists?'

'No.'

'It's probably as well for you that you didn't find it.'

'Why?'

'It would almost certainly have landed you in deeper trouble, that's why. More trouble than even you could have coped with. You're lucky to be back. Luckier than some!'

Chris gazed at him stonily. 'You know that Dimitriu was also in Bucharest?'

'Yes.'

'Tell me about that.'

'He held me prisoner. Later we had a fight and I escaped.'

'*You* and Dimitriu had a fight? Then what about Reyman?'

'I don't know anything about him.'

'You didn't see him there?'

'No. Should I have done?'

'I don't know. But it seems you're luckier than I thought you were. It may interest you to know that Reyman is being held in connection with Dimitriu's death.'

It was Chris' turn to register surprise. 'Dimitriu dead?'

'Yes.'

'It must be as a result of our fight. I mean, it was self-defence and all that; but what can I do about Reyman?'

'He hasn't yet been charged with anything, so he may be able to talk his way out of trouble. But that's his problem. It'll make him a bit more careful where he treads in future.' He fixed Chris with a hard look. 'Now, I want to hear about your dealings with old man Dimitriu. Incidentally, I suppose Janey's told you she found that cutting?' Chris nodded. 'Well, start at the beginning and tell me the lot.'

For the second time that evening, Chris described his meetings with Dimitriu. As he came to the final meeting he said, 'I've already told Janey that I didn't murder him and she believes me.'

'The jury believed you, too,' she broke in.

'Let's cut out the heroics,' Adams remarked, 'though if it'll help you to tell me the truth at last, I'll say that I believe you as well.'

'But do you really?'

'Certainly I do. I know who murdered him and it wasn't you.'

Chris shot bolt upright on the edge of the bed. 'Who did do it?'

'First, I want to hear your version of events,' Adams replied calmly.

Chris took a deep breath. 'It began just like our other meetings. He picked me up at Turnpike Lane Station and we drove out to the wood where it all happened. I suppose we'd been there about a quarter of an hour: he'd given me money for the trip and told me the exact location of the hidden gold when suddenly a hand with a revolver came through the window on my side and shot him at point-blank range. I was completely stunned: not even sure I wasn't dead myself. It seemed hours before I was able to gather my senses, but when I did, I couldn't get away quickly enough.'

'Did you realise that the murderer had dropped the gun – your gun – inside the car?'

'No. Or if I did, it failed to sink in. I was in too great a panic to think of anything except getting away.'

'You never caught sight of the person who fired the shot?'

'A gloved hand was all I saw.'

'I meant, afterwards?'

'No, nothing.'

There was a silence, then Adams said, 'A pity you didn't tell the truth at the outset.'

'A pity for whom?'

Sergeant Paget gave Chris a wry glance while Adams studiously ignored the rejoinder. It had been on the tip of his tongue to pile in with a lecture about possible perjury proceedings, but Chris' comment had stopped him. The point was well made, and, anyway, nobody was going to worry about perjury in these circumstances.

There ensued a further silence, this time broken by Chris.

'You promised to tell who did do the murder.'

'Can't you guess?'

'Was it Reyman?'

'No, Peter Dimitriu.'

XXVII

Adams was talking again. 'We were lucky in a way, since there's no better time for extracting the truth than when someone is in a state of emotional shock and Mrs Dimitriu was certainly that when we got to the house. She'd only just recovered from a faint brought on by news of her son's death and didn't have time to put on an act.

'The gist of what she told us was that the old man had been behaving so suspiciously that they began to wonder if he hadn't got another woman tucked away. From that it was only a short step to start worrying whether he mightn't be about to change his will. At all events, Peter Dimitriu followed his father on a couple of the occasions he met you, and this was enough to confirm their wildest fears. What on earth was he up to having a series of clandestine meetings with a young man who was a complete stranger! Incidentally, it was after the first occasion that Peter Dimitriu followed you home.'

'So it was he who stole my revolver?'

'That's the inference. I imagine he was also trying to find something out about you.'

'And Dimitriu who tipped you off anonymously on the phone?'

'Presumably.'

'What's going to happen to the old lady? Won't she be charged?'

'It's a question of evidence. She was sufficiently careful not to make any damaging admissions concerning her part. In fact she said that Peter only told her that it was he who'd shot his father on the eve of his departure for Bucharest. Until then, she'd believed it was you.'

'You don't believe that, do you?'

'No, but there isn't any evidence to prove otherwise. And by the time we see her again, I've no doubt she'll probably be denying we ever came to the house.' Adams shot out his legs and tilted his chair back against the wall. 'I said I'd dig out the truth and I have, despite everyone's efforts to conceal their bit of it.' He looked at Chris with a gleam in his eye. 'I don't suppose you want my advice, but I suggest you get yourself a regular job and do a spot of honest work.'

'I don't suppose you want mine either, so I shan't offer it! But as for a job, I do propose getting one, as I've got to have £100 as soon as possible.'

'Going to buy Janey a mink finger stall?'

'No, just support a girl in Paris.'

Janey remained silent at the time, but as soon as the officers had gone, she asked awkwardy, 'Is it true about a girl in Paris?'

Chris flung off his dressing-gown and jumped into bed. With a cheerful grin he said, 'You'll have to come over here if you want to find out.'